YULETIDE TALES OF HORROR

I0540166

Compiled & Edited by
NorGus Press

~

Jeffrey A. Angus
Stephanie K. Deal
Stacey Gilfus
Matt Nord

NorGus Press
Auburn, New York

Other Anthologies From NorGus Press

We dedicate this to all the elves that have labored for years for the fat man. For all the times they have had to stand in the shadows and haven't gotten the glory they deserve. The true heroes of the day.

We dedicated this to everyone that overeats at Christmas Parties and sings bawdy songs.

We dedicate this to kids everywhere who have taken a snowball in the kisser and who know the joy of the retaliation that will ensue.

We dedicate this to the people who just want their family to go away after Christmas dinner so they can take a nap.

We dedicate this to the ghost in all the Christmas stories.

~ NorGus Press

TABLE OF CONTENTS

NAUGHTY NAUGHTY
BY J. RODIMUS FOWLER

"My name is Jessup Leigh and I'm just a 'shit for brains' ol' country boy, born and raised in the Carolinas. I ain't got a lot of skills left that I'm still good at in my ripe old age of fifty-two. I can whip up a mean mess of beans and I can damn sure tell you a campfire story that'll make your bowels move faster than them ol' beans I was talking about. Anyway, sit down by the fire, take a load off and have a bowl of beans. I'm gonna tell you a story. Well, for those of you who have the fortitude or just the plain ol' morbid curiosity to stick around, it goes a lil' something like this..."

***

PART ONE - Xmas Eve in the House of Lost Expectations

It was the night before Christmas in the Town of Benson, North Carolina. More specifically, the Hollister's house on Dead Road. Rudy Jr. or "Lil' Rudy" as he was called because of his stature as well as his age, was prancing around the house like any other overexcited child waiting on Christmas morning. He was only eleven years old. His mother Shirley told him that if he didn't go to bed and be a good little boy Santa would just pass right by their house without stopping. No gifts and absolutely no Ho-Ho-Ho's.

1

Lil' Rudy tirelessly dragged his behind to bed and lay down under the covers. He kept one eye open as his mom cut out the lights and closed his door, leaving it cracked open just a little. His mom went to her room and shut the door. He heard the loud squeaking sound that the hinges always made and the click of the latch. For just a second, he thought that he also heard muffled voices through the thin plaster walls but he waited very still for a moment and all was quiet. He figured it was his mom humming a Christmas song the way she had been doing all night. He pulled the covers up tight and stared at the clock.

Rudy Sr. had been away on an extended business trip to procure some land up in the Virginias. It was Christmas Eve and he was going to make it home and surprise his beloved family. It had been almost two weeks since he had seen his son or felt his wife's loving embrace.

He lied to Shirley earlier that day when he had spoke with her on the phone; he told her he wouldn't be able to make it home until the day after Christmas and she sounded broken-hearted, but that's what he wanted so the surprise arrival would be spectacular. She mentioned to him that Rudy Jr. was going to be very upset if he woke up Christmas morning with his dad still out of town. Lil' Rudy had been looking forward to his return and talking about it all day. Rudy Sr. had a big bag of gifts and an even larger smile on his face. It was 11:38pm and he was almost home for the big surprise.

2

Work had been taking up a lot of his time the last few months and he felt like he was losing the tight bond he had with his family. He never had that growing up. When Rudy Sr. was a child his father would already be at work when he woke up and then at night when his father came home it would be so late that Rudy Sr. would already be asleep, unless he played possum just to see his dad come in the door, dog-tired and irritable. Many weeks of the year he would only see his father for breakfast on Sunday mornings. When Lil' Rudy was born he made a promise to himself to always be there for his family.

***

"Are ya'll still with me? You need a bathroom break or how bout' some more beans? They are mighty tasty if I do say so myself. Cause' I always use fresh meat! You sure? Alrighty then let's get back to the Hollister's..."

***

PART TWO – Lil' Rudy On the Top Step

It was two minutes to midnight. Lil' Rudy was too excited to sleep and was watching the hands of the clock spin around and around. Suddenly there was a noise from downstairs that sounded like the back door was opening.

Rudy Jr. crept out of bed as silent as a Christmas mouse. He opened up the bedroom door enough to squeeze his thin frame through the crack. Something or someone was definitely moving around downstairs; he heard footsteps. He walked across the hall to his parent's room door and twisted the iron knob. It was unlocked. He opened the door as quietly as he could but it made a distinct squeaking sound just as it started to move.

The door opened enough for Lil' Rudy to slip inside. He saw that his mom was sound asleep. The intrusion downstairs had not stirred her slumber. Lil' Rudy stuck his ear to the partially opened door and listened for anyone coming up the stairs. Apparently the squeaking hinge hadn't drawn any unwanted attention.

Lil' Rudy went over to his mom and gently nudged her on the shoulder to wake her up. She did not respond. He began to whisper in her ear, "Wake up, wake up!"

Still, there was no response; Lil' Rudy's mind began to race. He began to shake her more forcibly when her head lobbed over to one side and her mouth hung open with her tongue hideously dangling out. She was absolutely still.

The small boy began to panic in his very core. He slowly pulled the covers back and saw that his mother was lying in a pool of blood. She had deep wounds across her chest and stomach and large pieces of flesh from her torso were missing.

All of a sudden there was a loud crashing sound from downstairs that sounded like glass breaking. Lil' Rudy jumped with fright from the outburst, just in time to stop the shock from the horrors that lay before him from setting in.

Tears started to fall down the boys cheeks and he remembered what his dad had told him just before he went away. He told his son to take care of his mother and the house in his absence. He told Rudy Jr. that he was now the man of the house!

The boy stood there staring at the door crying silent tears. He was so scared that he wet his pajamas. He had failed his dad's request and let something happen to his mother. Lil' Rudy felt sadness, disappointment, humiliation and an extreme anger welling up inside.

Rudy Jr. turned and looked at his mother and wiped the tears from his eyes. His anger was in control now, someone had hurt his mother and they were still in the house. He went to the cabinet where his dad kept the rifle that he was never supposed to touch. But he had touched it before, many times. It was one of his favorite things to sneak out and show his friends when his parents weren't looking. It made him feel special to show off the gun in front of his pals. He even knew how to shoot it because his father had taken him hunting for squirrels twice and had practiced shooting bottles with him three times.

Lil' Rudy grabbed the gun, pulled the bolt action lever back and reset it with a chambered .22 caliber bullet. He wiped more tears from his eyes but they just kept filling back up, then he walked out the door and stood on the top step looking down into the darkness and the shadows below.

5

***

"Ol' Jessup here, just wondering if you needed me to check your pulse? One time I told this story and a man just fell over, still as a stone he was. The young feller just fainted right there in the very same spot that you are sitting right now. Sure you're OK? Alright, here we go..."

***

PART THREE – Seasoned Greetings

The noises downstairs were like someone sweeping glass across wood with the occasional sounds of a man grunting. The grunting scared the dickens out of Lil' Rudy. It made him think of pigs eating out of a trough. He remembered the terrifying grunting from when he went on a field trip with the school to a real farm that had horses, chickens, cows and pigs. The vulgar sounds of the pigs had stayed with the small boy.

Lil' Rudy's hands began to shake and tears ran down both of his puffy cheeks more fluently. He mustered up all his courage, looked down the barrel of the gun and called out, "Come out who ever you are!"

The sweeping noises stopped and the house sat still for what felt like minutes. A darker shade of black than the rest of the darkness moved into view. The boy's eyes began to adjust to the dim lighting. He saw the shape of a fat man at the bottom of the stairs slowly beginning to move up the steps. The sounds of the pigs eating filled his mind.

Rudy Sr., who had just broken a drinking glass and was struggling to reach the mess wearing his fat Santa suit, heard his son and walked over to the foyer and looked up the steps into the darkness above. His eyes were more adjusted to the darkness; he saw his son standing there with tears rolling down his face and started up the steps.

He was about to say *what's wrong*, but he only got out one syllable before the gun went off.

Lil' Rudy squeezed the trigger, careful not to pull it, *something his father taught him*_and the gun went off. The bullet struck Rudy Sr. in the upper jaw and ricocheted up into his skull penetrating his brain, dropping him immediately to the floor. He fell over and landed in a heap at the bottom of the steps.

Lil' Rudy carefully moved down the steps one at a time, looking for movement from the *Boogie Man* below. When he reached the light switch on the wall at the bottom of the stairs, he flipped it on and saw the horrors that lay at his feet. The gun fell from Lil' Rudy's hands and landed on the hardwood floor with a loud smack. The boy was definitely in shock now gazing down at his father's corpse.

The squeaking from his parent's bedroom door sounded out through the silence. Frozen in place, the boy stared back up at the top of the steps as a dark figure appeared from the blackness. A low raspy voice cried out.

"Naughty naughty, little boy!"

A large hulking shadow started down the steps very slowly; each time the large man moved to a new step, the creaking of the hardwood sent a chill down Lil' Rudy's spine. The little boy's body actually twitched with each step.

Rudy Jr., still stuck in the horror of his parent's death, just stood there watching as the big man descended the stairs into the light, closer and closer to the boy. Even though his ears were still ringing from the gun shot and the creaking steps were almost driving him mad, the eerie voice penetrated his mind once again.

"I've read my list and checked it twice!"

The frightened little boy had a brief moment of clarity and reached down for the rifle. He flipped back the lever and chambered it again. When he raised it up at the man, it was too late. The big man was already right on top of him and grabbed the gun from his tiny trembling hands.

Lil' Rudy began to cry and screamed as loud as he could. The big man back-handed the boy across the face, knocking him across the room and sending him crashing to the floor. Before Lil' Rudy could even come back to his senses, the man was standing above his small, battered frame.

The man picked Rudy up in the air like he weighed no more

than a sack of potatoes and pulled him close to meet his eyes. The big man had blood caked up on his white beard and dripping from the corners of his mouth. He had golden yellow, blood stained teeth and the foulest smelling breath that Lil' Rudy had ever encountered. It reminded him of the scent coming from the dead turtle that he had stumbled onto by the pond out back last year, but worse.

The man had dark eyes that were sunk way back in his skull and the most menacing of stares. His eyes pierced through the boy like a razor through flesh.

He leaned in closer to Lil' Rudy and the boy could feel the wretched warmness of his breath. The raspy voice bellowed out, spitting blood in the boys face as it spoke.

"You didn't leave out any snacks for me! So I had to make my own. Your mother was almost as sweet as a new born baby and I think you'll be even tastier! I have always loved fresh meat way more than cookies and milk, especially during the Holidays. Merry Christmas you naughty lil' boy!"

The man's mouth opened wide as he leaned in even closer to the boys face. The stench of the man's breath filled the boy's nostrils again and he almost gagged. A stream of urine ran down the boy's leg as Lil' Rudy began to scream.

No one ever heard his short lived cries.

The big man pulled out the blood stained meat cleaver that was tucked in his belt, started humming *Deck the Halls* and began to carve the holiday meat. He stuffed his gifts from the Hollister's into a large burlap sack, threw it over his shoulder and walked right out the front door.

It was going to be a merry Christmas after all.

***

"There, there now don't be scared. Ol' Jessup ain't gonna hurt you. Wait a minute, where are you going? Ain't no need to rush off like that. There's plenty of beans to go around and I made em' with the freshest of meats! I just got through telling this story a couple of hours ago to these two blonde girls that came through here. Hey you, enough of that! Quit wasting my meat. Why are you vomiting like that, were they friends of yours?"

WONDERFUL
BY MARC SORONDO

James Simmons had decided to kill himself. In his opinion the part of his life worth living had long passed and for years now he'd been forcing himself through Hell without even being judged. He'd decided not to do it anymore.

He walked out onto the George Washington Bridge, stopping only when he was right between New York and New Jersey. He liked the idea that maybe, just maybe, there'd be problems with reporting his death because they wouldn't know which state to put on the forms.

As he walked out over the water, the Hudson wind pulling at his hair and clothes, he itemized his life, double-checking to make sure that he hadn't overlooked some good or redeemable quality, making sure that he truly did not have a reason to live anymore.

He blamed it, at least partly, on money. He'd never had much and never seemed to be able to hold on to it when he did. For James, trying to save money was like trying to hold a gust of wind: he never could hold it and couldn't ever be sure he'd really had it in the first place.

His money problems, once a problem separate and apart from the others, had tainted all the other aspects of his life. He tried not to blame it all on money. He'd heard what people said about money not buying happiness, but he'd also learned that the lack thereof could ensure that happiness kept its distance.

James leaned onto the railing, his elbows on the dirty metal, and spit out over the water, where the cold wind caught everything and pulled it away. He looked down at the water, black and glossy as polished onyx, reflecting the moonlight.

Maureen didn't love him anymore; he knew that. Sometimes he wondered if she'd ever cheated on him, but realized that, of course, she hadn't. She spent all of her time working two terrible paying jobs only to come home exhausted and sleep. She had no time for affairs. She wasn't the type anyway, James knew. Though a little part of him wanted her to be, wanted to put some of the blame for his unhappiness on Maureen for infidelity or drugs or some other terrible vice, he knew he couldn't. She was a good person…a hard worker…responsible. She'd have been better off if she'd never met James, he was sure of that.

He didn't lose her love to another man or addiction; instead, she began to see him for the waste that he was…instead he lost her love to nothing at all.

If he died, maybe she could start over. Maybe then she could make the best of what time she had left, what time she hadn't wasted with him.

He carried a knife along with his empty wallet. He wasn't sure if he should try to make it look like a mugging gone wrong rather than a suicide. He wasn't sure if that would make the news easier or harder to accept.

"How can you be sure things would be better without you?" a voice said behind him.

James turned quickly, startled to see an older man that had somehow managed to get right behind him without his noticing. He had a thin build, a bit less than six feet, with thick, grey hair and Italian features.

A car was pulled to the side of the right lane with its hazard lights flashing.

For an instant he considered pulling the knife but quickly realized that the old guy was no mugger...and shortly after that he realized it would be stupid to defend himself only to then kill himself.

"What are you talking about?"

"Come on. I know what you're planning to do." The old guy smiled a little.

Something about that smile made James believe that he really did know what he'd planned to do and maybe even the circumstances that had led up to that decision.

"What makes you so sure that this would be a better world without you in it?"

"If you knew me better..." James started.

"I know enough," the old man said, flashing a smile that made James think of Hollywood...classic Hollywood. It was the smile a leading man would have smiled in an old black-and-white movie.

"Yeah, well...it couldn't be any worse without me."

"What if I said I could show you?"

"Oh, man...alright, old-timer. Save the Christmas movie bullshit for someone else."

13

"Do you really think killing yourself will give Maureen a chance to...'start over.' That it'll wipe the slate clean and she'll just pick up and move on over to Park Avenue?"

James mouth moved as he searched for something to say.

"You're completely broke and you've got some of the worst life insurance in existence...which, by the way, won't pay a dime if you kill yourself. What does your death offer her? Hmmm...aside from a chance to go through a fairly miserable life completely alone?"

"How could you possibly know...?"

"I just know. And like I've already said, I can show you if you'd like. You can make sure that you are making an educated decision in knifing yourself and jumping off the bridge."

"Alright...show me." He couldn't believe he'd said it, couldn't believe that even part of him actually expected to see, that he believed the old nut.

The old man extended his hand. "Name's Lou," he said. "Let's get moving."

James shook Lou's hand and followed him to his car, a mundane sedan, painted a light blue that looked silver in the light from the bridge.

As the occasional late night commuter drove past, flashing angry looks at the hazards on the sedan, Lou walked around to the driver's side door, apparently fearless even as angry drivers whizzed past in sports cars and SUV's that would spray him all over the asphalt if they hit him.

"Get in," Lou said, carelessly throwing open his own

14

door as wide as the hinges would allow. He slid into the seat and waited a moment before pulling the door closed.

James got in, feeling like he never should have let the old loon stop him, like he should have just jumped and ended the whole mess already.

There was a faint scent of cheap air-freshener, something floral, along with the musty, ash smell of a smoker's car.

"So where would you like to go?" Lou asked pleasantly. He pulled a box of Marlboro's from the center console and popped one into his mouth.

James sat, staring at the old guy, not answering his question.

Lou held out the pack, offering.

"No thanks. I quit a long time ago. Too expensive."

"Alright then...let's hear it. Where are we going?" Lou insisted. He started to fiddle with the radio, scanning stations too quickly for James to hear what was on them.

"Home, I guess," James finally answered.

Lou stopped abruptly on a station playing Frank Sinatra. "Chairman of the board," he said with a smile that held his cigarette clamped between his teeth. "217 Central, coming right up."

"That's not my address," James said. "I'm on Main. 346. Shouldn't you know that?"

"346 Main," Lou said with a smoky exhale. "Whatever you say."

"Why don't you know my address if you know so much about me?" James asked. Now that they were in the car, that he was, in a sense, in Lou's control, he was getting nervous. He knew he shouldn't worry. Hell, he was about to kill himself anyway. What could this old guy do that was any worse?

"There are worse things," Lou said, looking at him from the corner of his eye. He blew smoke towards the slightly opened window. "But I'm telling you the truth. I just want to show you how things would be if you'd never been born."

"Yeah, I'm familiar with the premise," James said as the car turned off Route 46 and onto Main Street. "I watch it once a year in December."

Lou slowed and pulled the car over. "346," he announced.

James opened the door and extended his right leg. "You're not coming?"

"I'll wait here. Go check it out, and when you're done, I'll take you wherever else you want to go."

James shrugged and got out of the car. He ran up a few familiar steps and slid his key into the front door. He turned the knob with the key, waiting for the door to stick. The door stuck every time, had since they'd first moved in, and he'd always meant to fix it.

The door swung open with a slight creek, but smoothly, without the slightest resistance.

James walked in and was greeted by pale yellow walls rather than the light green he'd expected. Photos lined the walls, every one of a stranger.

"Billy? Is that you?" a woman's voice called from the

16

kitchen.

James panicked, stepped backwards out the door, and pulled it closed. He hopped down the few front steps in one leap and got into Lou's car as fast as he could.

"Either you're not crazy or I am," James said.

Lou sat their smiling at him, the car's engine idling. The front door of 346 Main Street opened and a tall, older woman with dark hair and gray roots poked her head out. She scanned the street and spotted the blue sedan with the two men in it.

"Shit. Get us out of here," James ordered.

"Sure. Where to?" Lou asked nonchalantly.

"Just hurry before she calls the cops."

"Okay. Where would you like to go?"

James tried to remember the address Lou had mentioned earlier and found that he couldn't. So he said his mother's address, that of his childhood home. "74 Park Street."

The house was only a few blocks away, and Lou treated speed limits like suggestions. They reached the house in seconds.

Although it was clearly the right address, according to its positioning and the gold 74 that hung against the white backdrop of the front door, the house was not the one in which he'd grown up.

What had once been a small, 1950's style split-level, was now a huge home that dwarfed the small plot of suburban property on which it'd been built. Though James could see aspects of the old house shining through (the big window in the front that looked out on his mother's flower garden; the porch that curved from the front door around the left-hand corner and towards the back of the house), this home was three floors and extended out into what had been the side yard when he'd been growing up. At the front, right-hand corner was an octagonal addition that, James could see through a window, was home to a huge tree covered in gold lights and silver decorations. Two white columns spiraled in gold garland framed the door.

"What the hell?" James said to himself as he walked up the concrete path that led through the landscaped front yard to the door. He ascended the two steps to the front door slowly, unable to shake the idea that he'd finally snapped and he was imagining all of this.

James tried his key and found it didn't work. He rang the bell and waited, glancing briefly over his shoulder at Lou, who sat in the idling car mouthing the words to some Tony Bennett song that could barely be heard where James stood. He waved at James through the smoke that filled the car and seeped out of its cracked-open windows.

"What am I doing?" James whispered to himself. Then he heard the thump of approaching feet. His mother must have been feeling good today; her steps were quicker than they'd been in years.

The lock clicked and the door opened.

It was his mother, but it wasn't. She wore a bright blouse and pants with a tropical print. She was a good 40 pounds lighter than his mother and had long hair, pulled back in a braid.

18

"Ma? What the hell is going on?" James blurted out.

"Excuse me?" She said, sliding over a bit to position the door in between them as much as possible.

"Mom?" James ventured.

"I'm sorry. You must be mistaken."

"Mom, it's me."

"You've got the wrong house," she said, louder.

"Honey! Something wrong?!" A sturdy male voice called from upstairs. More footsteps came from above.

"Who the hell is that?" James asked, forcing himself through the hardly opened door.

"Honey?" The voice called again. It was close now.

And then, as if it took her a moment to realize James had forced his way into the house, his mother screamed.

The footsteps from upstairs came faster now, and James headed up to meet them. He only made it up the first few steps before a man reached the landing above him.

"Dad?" James asked, his voice starting to waver.

It hit him like a gunshot to the belly. He couldn't breathe for a moment. His father…alive.

"I don't know who the hell you are, but you'd better get out of here before the cops show up," he screamed. He pointed to his wife, telling her to call 911 with an angry gesture.

"But…Dad?" James said again.

"Listen, pal. I can see you're confused, and I feel bad, I really do, but I've got one son, and you're not him…so you'd better leave."

"You don't understand," James said.

"Get out now!" his father screamed while pointing at the still open front door.

James slowly walked to the door. It slammed shut just as he passed it, and he could hear the deadbolt slide home through it.

He walked back to the car and got in.

"What's the matter?" Lou asked.

"My dad's alive...my mom's healthy...their house...my old house..." James said.

"That was never your house," Lou corrected. "You've never had a home. You've never been born. You don't exist here."

"What happened? How is my dad...?"

"Not dead with a chunk of cancer in his brain?"

James turned to scowl at Lou.

"Hey, don't get offended. You can't get offended. It never happened now," Lou said.

"But why didn't it happen? It's not like I gave him cancer."

"Long story short," Lou started, "you were never born. Thus, your younger brother Henry was an only child. The few resources your parents had, as well as all of their attention, went to him. Thus his grades were better. The scholarships from those grades and your ex-parents' savings got Henry through college. He got himself through law school. Henry is, in this reality, one of the most well known legal figures on the East Coast, so you can imagine the kind of money he makes. He wanted to buy your parents a big new home, but they couldn't bear to leave 'their home' so he built it up for them and let them retire early. He made sure they saw the best doctors, so your father's cancer was caught early, before it could spread, and treated effectively."

Lou stopped for a moment, and then added, "Oh, and he's sending them to Hawaii for Christmas."

James stared up at the huge house. Then sirens became audible.

"Oops, my least favorite people are coming. Where to now?"

James couldn't think. He just stared up at that huge house. He hated it. It represented everything that his parents would have enjoyed if they'd never had him.

"You did want to see, didn't you? You did want to be sure that the world would be better without you, right?" Lou asked.

"It wasn't supposed to be..." James said.

"Says who? Come on, what else do you want to see?"

James was torn between Henry and Maureen. Then he decided, "Take me to Hank's house." He was going to apologize to his brother, even though he wasn't his brother anymore. He'd apologize and tell him how proud he was. Even though Hank would think he was crazy, even though he wouldn't recognize him, James felt it was something he had to do.

Then he would kill himself. He'd do it here, to let this better world go on without his influence to ruin it for the few people he'd ever cared about.

"Not your wife?" Lou asked as he pulled slowly away. The lights on the police cars were visible in the rear-view mirror as they rounded the corner at the end of the block and sped towards number 74.

"No." He couldn't bare it. Seeing his parents was bad enough. He couldn't stand to see how much better Maureen had turned out without him. He had loved her, and sometimes he still did. Convincing himself that the woman he loved would be better off without him was bad enough, but knowing it as fact...

"You know, if I'm going to be honest with you in this, if I'm going to actually let you see how things would be without you, there's something I should tell you about Maureen?"

"No. I'm sure she's better off without me too."

"That's the thing..." Lou started.

"She's not better off?"

"She is. I just think you might..."

"No," James said. "I don't want to know. She's happier this way. They all are. I just want to see my brother. Then we're done."

"So...you still plan on doing it?" Lou asked.

James looked out the window silently.

"Oh-kay," Lou said. He played with the radio again. James was just about to say that he couldn't bare another Italian crooner, when Lou stopped on "Under My Thumb" by the Stones.

"Love the Stones," Lou said. His smile had returned. "They may be my favorite band."

James sighed. "Wouldn't have thought that before, with the Sinatra and stuff," he said, his gaze never leaving the window.

"What can I say, I've got eclectic tastes," Lou said. He slid another cigarette from the bright red pack and placed it between his lips. He lit it and took a long, slow pull. "Sure you don't want one?" he asked with a smile.

James thought about how hard it had been to quite all those years ago. How he'd managed not to take even a single drag in over ten years. He thought about going through the hell of quitting all over again.

Just as James was about to decline, Lou said, "You don't exist, and you're going to kill yourself anyway. What's a smoke going to hurt?"

James snatched one out of the pack and lit it. He coughed for a few seconds, but then the nicotine hit him, caressed his nerves like an old lover, and eased his tension and his mind like an opiate.

"Fucking missed these," James said. "Every day, for years, I've missed them."

"So have them," Lou said, grinning at him. He inhaled and the smoldering cigarette cast a red glow in his eyes. "Think of this as an opportunity. Why should they all get this chance at happiness and you don't?"

"What?"

"Think of the possibilities you have before you right now. You've been faithful to your wife through the whole mess of your marriage; you're going to honestly tell me you've never wanted to have sex with another woman?"

"Are you serious?" James asked. "Are you kidding? The whole reason everyone I care about is happy right now is because I wasn't around to fuck it all up for them. You think…"

Lou's grin changed, but never for a moment left. "Don't get so pissy. Just think about it…that's all. I've let you tread where you don't belong, and that makes you a very powerful man here."

"You listen—"

"217 Central," Lou announced, cutting James off as he slammed on the brakes. He stopped in front of a huge house; a building that James thought should be called an estate or a manor.

Lou had stopped the car at the edge of Henry's property, between the two entrances to a large circular driveway. A marble lion crouched just to the side of the car on the picture perfect lawn inside the asphalt semicircle.

"Now that's just tacky," Lou said. "Guy makes a few million and he wants a marble menagerie on his property."

That was nothing compared to the Roman columns that stood like sentries before the front entrance to the house, holding up a large balcony that James assumed led off some lavish master bedroom.

The whole house was littered with elements of classical architecture. There was even a stained glass window depicting the birth of Athena from the forehead of Zeus over the balcony.

"Talk about money changing you," Lou said.

James grinned. "Hank was into Kiss growing up. He painted his face black and white every year on Halloween. His idea of artwork had been band posters and pin-ups. How could this be the same guy?"

"He's not," Lou said. "You don't seem to be getting that."

"I get it. It's just hard to."

James got out of the car and, running the tips of his fingers over the cool marble surface of the crouched lion as he passed it, headed for the front door.

Upon reaching the door, he found himself fighting an urge to turn back. He didn't know what good it would do him to see Hank. It was a sad attempt at getting some closure, he knew, but he would say his piece. He would apologize for ruining a life that no longer existed in a past that was imaginary everywhere but in his own mind.

James pressed the doorbell and listened to an unfamiliar tune played by the struck chimes.

The moment he waited seemed to drag out, accompanied by the fading tone of the doorbell's final note.

Then the door opened.

And it was Maureen who'd opened it. Maureen as she'd been when they'd first fallen in love, before life had gotten a hold of her and beaten her. Before he'd come into her life to ruin it. There were no crow's feet or bags under her eyes. Her face, as well as her body, was slim and firm and youthful.

The she smiled at him, a bit perplexed, and it broke his heart.

"Maureen?" It came out more as a sad declaration than a question.

She continued to smile, but James could see on her face

25

that she was trying to place him, to come up with his name or a recollection of why she should know him.

"I'm sorry. I'm usually good about this. How do I know you, Mr...?"

A voice in James' head screamed, *You don't know me?! I'm your husband!* It wasn't his voice, but it was a familiar one.

"Um, James, and you don't, technically. I was looking for Hank, and..." James said.

Maureen laughed and the sound of it made James want to throw up.

"I don't think I've ever heard anyone other than Henry's parents call him that."

"Oh...that's what I've always called him," James said.

"Well, he worked late tonight. He's got a big trial coming up. But he's on his way home if you want to wait for him. He called a few minutes ago and said he was close."

"Sure," James said after a pause. "I guess that'll work."

Maureen stepped aside from the doorway, and James entered through a cloud of her perfume. It was a scent that he'd never associated with her: a light, sweet smell in no way similar to the cheap perfume she'd always worn.

"Would you like a cup of coffee?" she asked, already heading for the kitchen down the hall.

James followed her, scanning her from head to toe, amazed by the shape of her body under the jeans and t-shirt she was wearing. She was built like a 20-year-old.

"So how do you know Henry?" she asked as she entered the kitchen.

"I've known him since we were kids," James said,

truthfully enough. "But I haven't seen him in…god. He's probably unrecognizable now."

"It's bittersweet, isn't it?" She smiled again. "To go home again, but see it's so different?"

"Painful," James muttered.

"How have we never met before? You weren't at our wedding, Mr. James?"

"Oh, James is my first name." That hurt. "I hadn't seen Hank in so long at that point, and I was going through a few…things."

"Hmmm…that's too bad. Cream and sugar?"

"Please. Actually, could I use your bathroom before the coffee?"

"Of course. Second door on the left, back the way we came in."

James thanked her again and hurried to the bathroom. He splashed cold water on his face. "How are they together?" he whispered to himself. He fought the urge to cry and then the urge to vomit.

Think about it, the same voice in his head started. He recognized it this time. It was Lou's. *You met her because her mother and your mother were friends and you two were about the same age. With you out of the picture, she went with Henry…the rest is obvious.*

James shook his head.

You think she could never think of your brother that way? You think she never did? You think she didn't find him attractive, didn't fantasize about him?

James splashed more water on his face.

27

He couldn't figure out how things had gone so wrong, how he'd become such a stain on everyone else's lives.

You got screwed, that's how. Some people just get dealt a shitty hand in life, and you, my friend, were dealt a hand like a foot.

James turned off the water, wiped his face on a yellow, decorative towel, and headed back for the kitchen.

James found Maureen sitting at the kitchen table, a steaming cup of coffee in front of her and another opposite her.

"Okay?" she said flashing him a smile as he sat across from her.

"Fine," he said. He tried to flash a smile in return, but it felt more like a snarl to him. "I've just had a very long day."

"The trip itself? Traffic?"

"No. I'm actually here on business." James interrupted himself for a quick sip of coffee. "But the business part of the trip isn't working out so well."

"I'm sorry to hear that."

"I was hoping that seeing Hank would help. He's become so successful in the years since we've fallen out of touch, I thought seeing a real happy ending would do me some good."

Maureen blushed and it was angelic. "Wow. That's kind of sweet. I never thought of our life as such a happy ending before...not that we're not happy," she stumbled, "just that I never think of it as an ending...still a work in progress."

Maybe she's got doubts, Lou's voice said in his mind like a conscience. *Not so happy after all?*

James leaned in towards Maureen. "Can I ask you

28

something?" he whispered.

"Sure," she whispered back, grinning impishly. She leaned in as well.

"Do you still love him?"

"Of course I do," she laughed.

"Have you always? Never doubted?"

"We've had rough patches. Every marriage does, but I've always known he was the right man for me...why do you ask?"

James closed his eyes for a moment, and heard echoes from Maureen's marriage in his life, his reality, the one he'd ruined. He heard her crying...heard her sobbing...and when he finally had silence, he knew he heard her acceptance, acceptance that it was ruined, acceptance that it was too late.

Maureen reached out and put her hand on his, gave it a gentle squeeze, and asked, "Are you sure you're alright?"

James opened his eyes and a tear rolled down his cheek. "I love you. No matter how bad things got, I always have."

Maureen's concern fell apart into confusion. She pulled her hand away. "I don't understand."

"Some part of me always thought you were the only thing I'd gotten right. Somewhere, deep down, I thought you'd been the one thing I did right, even if the rightness didn't last. I should have told you once in a while, I guess..."

"James," she interrupted.

"But now I find out that you were the biggest mistake of all." He reached out to grab her hand, but she pulled it away before he'd reached it.

29

She stood from her stool, took a step back, never taking her frightened eyes from him.

"I ruined you." James wiped at his eyes.

"I think you should go."

"No. I wasn't trying to scare you...I wasn't even looking for you. I wanted to see Hank...to tell him I was sorry, and..."

"You should leave," Maureen said.

He stood and took a step towards her. She matched it with a step back.

"Don't be scared. I'm not crazy, it's just..."

"Get out!" she screamed. The way she screamed, the stern, angry way she'd screamed those words, made him think of his father screaming the very same thing.

Your dead father, Lou whispered musically in his head. *And this is supposed to be your wife. What's left for you when you don't exist, Jimmy?*

"You'd better leave before Henry gets home. He'll be here soon and if he sees you scaring me..."

James felt his entire universe compressing, all existence as he'd known it being crushed into the infinitesimally small, and then further, into nothing at all.

He stepped towards Maureen again, and she stepped back, backing herself up against the refrigerator.

Her eyes darted to the left.

James knew she was planning to dash to the side and run, probably screaming, from the house.

He reached out and snatched her arm.

Now the real screaming began. The volume of it hit

30

James in the face like a slap.

He grabbed her throat with his free hand and squeezed, just hard enough to quiet her, to make her voice raspy and small. It was still loud enough, he thought, to be heard by neighbors or someone walking past.

He brought his other hand from her arm to her throat and squeezed with both.

Now she was silent. She scratched at his face with her manicured nails, aiming for his eyes but just tearing into his forehead, his cheeks.

She was getting weak, her legs wobbling before finally giving out.

James guided her body to the floor gently, and, looming over her, continued to squeeze, to hold down the scream that still wanted to come.

She clawed at his face again, gauging skin away.

Blood from his wounds dripped onto her face, into her bulging, open eyes.

"You love me," James said. "You love *me*." He repeated it again and again. He wanted to cry, to weep, but he wouldn't let himself. The drops of falling blood would have to serve as his tears.

And then it was over. Her face, which had slowly turned pink and then red, now turned a purplish-blue. Her struggling stopped. The pressure of a scream fighting to escape left her throat.

"You love me," he said a final time. An unwelcome tear fell and mixed with his blood on her face.

James heard a key engage the lock on the front door.

He looked quickly around, and headed left, the way Maureen had tried to go, into the dining room.

Henry Simmons, in an expensive suit, smiling an expensive smile, walked into his house and was greeted with the sight of his wife's feet on the floor, the rest of her body obscured by the kitchen table. He dropped his briefcase and was already running down the hall when it hit the floor with a soft thud.

He dropped hard to his knees on the tile floor of the kitchen; his hands hovering over Maureen's body as if he worried touching her would do more damage. He put his hand to her cheek, finally, but quickly pulled it away when he felt how cold it was.

James could see Henry kneeling over her, saw the tears fall from his eyes and patter onto her t-shirt. Then all of a sudden Hank started fumbling in his pocket. James looked around and grabbed the first sturdy object that he could find: a small candlestick off the dining room table.

James stepped into the threshold between the kitchen and dining room just as Henry pulled a cell phone from his pocket.

"I'm sorry, Hank," James said monotonously. But he wasn't...not anymore. He'd been dealt a downright shitty hand. It hadn't been his fault.

As Henry's gaze reached his face, James snarled and brought the candlestick down on Henry's forehead.

Henry fell, but immediately starting moaning and pushing himself back up.

"You bastard," he mumbled as he drooled onto the tile

32

next to Maureen. "Killed her…" He sobbed now. "…bastard."

James hit him again, in the back of the head, and Henry dropped face first onto the tile.

Henry's right hand lashed out, clutching James' pants, gripping them with more strength than James' brother had ever had.

"Maureen…" Henry sobbed quietly, his face still against the tile.

James could hear it in Henry's lament, some quality to his dying words that revealed that he was already dead, had been since he'd felt her lifeless cheek…something that gave away that they'd been in love, that they had been the right match and one couldn't go on without the other.

James heard this…and it mocked him. It insulted his very existence.

"Ruined…" James said. He brought the candlestick down on Henry's head, smashing it against the tile. Then again. The third time James heard a crack. Either Henry's skull or the tile beneath it had broken.

James shook off the now loose hand clutching his pant leg and dropped the candlestick to the floor.

His fingerprints and blood were everywhere, but he could care less. He didn't exist here. His files and records were on the other side of the bridge.

He walked outside, closing the door behind him, and saw the light blue sedan idling right where he'd left it. The windows were down and light grey tobacco smoke drifted from them. He could hear music faintly, but could not recognize the song.

He got in the car and immediately took a cigarette from Lou's pack and lit it.

Smiling as always, Lou said, "Well, you've looked better."

"Fuck you," James said, the cigarette dangling from between his lips.

Lou chuckled. "That's the spirit. I knew there was still some life left in you."

James took a deep drag, deep enough to burn his lungs.

"So what's next, Jimmy? You want to kill your parents?" Lou asked as he changed gear from park to drive. "Burn a school full of kids? Blow up a building? There's a pretty good President right now. Up for an assassination?"

"I don't know."

"Well, what do you know?" Lou asked. He turned up the volume on the radio. The song James couldn't make out earlier was Led Zepplin's version of "When the Levee Breaks."

James smiled, cigarette smoke rising and curling around his bloody face before being sucked out the car window. He looked at Lou, took another huge drag, and said, "I'll ruin everything. It seems that's what I do."

Smiling, drumming his fingers on the steering wheel to the slow beat of the song, Lou drove out into the night, towards whatever was coming next.

34

HOME ALONE WITH THE ZOMBIES ON 34TH STREET
BY ROBERT FREESE

"Santa...Santaaaa..." The voice was gravelly, strained. The word was pushed from the undead elf's cracked, bloody lips. "Santaaaa..." Breathless, the name was spat repeatedly from dead lungs from the other side of the office door. Others joined in, each repeating the fat man's name.

Their dead little hands scratched and beat on the door's outer surface. Nails gouging the wood, snapping off until the ends of their fingers were little more than bloody stubs, but still the living dead elves continued their frantic activity. They knew the big guy was in the office.

"Santa..."

How many were there? Santa wondered, sitting at his desk. He tried to figure how many elves were possibly left. *What was the last census?* I didn't matter. Between the ones who had been outright killed and ripped to pieces, and the ones that had sustained only minimal damage and returned to life, albeit an obscene parody of life, there probably wasn't but a handful of living elves left.

Once they came back to life nothing seemed to stop them. Santa had used the Mossberg SA-20 Autoloader the boys on the production line presented to him for his birthday

35

last year to blow the heads off the invading zombies, but no sooner did their heads explode then their little elfin bodies struggled for balance and got back up. Many had been blown completely in half with the 20 gauge loads, only for both halves to continue moving around with spastic life.

"Santa..."

They continued chanting his name. It was maddening. Their deep, dead mantra was drowning out even the blasting arctic winds.

"Santa..."

The Mossberg lie empty on the floor next to the desk. There were no more shells, at least no more shells to which he had access. Not that it mattered.

"Santa..."

It had all started less than thirty-six hours ago. It seemed that every corpse in the world just came back to life and started attacking the living. They didn't so much eat the living than tear their bodies to shreds. To do this they used whatever they could, including their teeth. It was happening everywhere. Within twenty-four hours communication all over the world had been shut down.

At the North Pole, the icy graves of the Christmas Memorial Cemetery gave monstrous birth to the living dead abominations. The reanimated corpses of the deceased elves attacked the reindeer stables first and then moved into Christmas Town. When the living survivors tried to seek safety in the giant toy factory, they were overwhelmed by the dead before the factory could be properly fortified.

The stables were like a slaughterhouse. Blood and

innards dripped from everywhere and everything. Only Rudolph got away, but not unscathed. Although not ripped to pieces, the red nosed reindeer sustained enough damage that he laid down and died, then instantly awoke as one of them. Rudolph's shiny nose glowed demonically red in the icy cold polar night.

"Santa…"

They had been glued to the news like the rest of the world, watching newscasts from all over before everything was shut down. Initially they tried to fortify the Christmas castle and some of the specialty workshops, but the big factory was the only place to really house everyone. The elves worked together as if on a Christmas Eve deadline, but the factory could not be fortified fast enough. The army of undead elves worked faster to find every chink in the makeshift armor. The dead ones were smart. They got into the factory through a tunnel in the basement. When the dead entered the factory the living didn't know what hit them.

"Santa…Santaaaa…"

For as long as he lived, which he didn't think would be all that long now, Santa would never forget the screams of Winifred as she was attacked and torn to pieces. If there was anything to be thankful for it was that there had not been enough of his wife left to come back to life like some of the others.

"Santa…" The voices continued croaking his name over and over again.

Pouring the last of the whiskey from the decanter he kept in his desk into an oversized stein, he drank it down in one fast gulp. It burned a freight train path straight to his belly. Usually he indulged only when another successful run had been completed. This year he was drinking so he would have the courage to do what needed to be done.

"Santa…"

"You little bastards aren't going to get me!" He raised the Smith & Wesson 632 revolver to his forehead. He hoped to God the .327 Federal Magnum slug would tear through his brain and kill him instantly rather than ricocheting around his skull and leaving him lying on the floor bleeding to death. It happened. He had seen a lot of good kids go down that path when they got older. Things didn't always work out the way they thought they would. He prayed that his luck would be in this one shot.

He wanted only to be reunited with his wife.

"Santa…"

Would he be like them? Would he get up and walk around, living but dead? Would he help find and then kill the last remaining living elves? Would he have any memories of who he was, of what happened? Would there be any pain?

Ultimately, who cared? It was a good bet there was no one left living at the North Pole to hurt. It was a dead place, now. What was one more walking corpse?

"Santa…Santa….Santaaaa…."

"I'll see you little bastards in hell!"

Just as his finger began tightening around the trigger the office door shattered inward with a thunderous crash. The living dead elves spilled through the splintered pieces of wood, crawling over one another to get to the warm body sitting behind the desk.

Teeth caked with blood and raw meat, eyes glowing bright yellow, the undead elves were in a rush to consume the once jolly fat man.

"Santa!" Their voices croaked as one.

A single tear rolled down Santa's rosy cheek. He pulled the hammer back and put the muzzle of the 632 revolver in his mouth.

Don't let them tear me to pieces.

The millisecond before he pulled the trigger a tingling sensation filled his body. It was like when he slept wrong and his arm fell to sleep, feeling heavy and tingly from the loss of circulation, only now it was his entire body. He even felt it in his heart, as if something was tugging him forward.

A loud crack of thunder filled the office.

The revolver?

In a puff of smoke, Santa disappeared from the factory office as the undead elves rushed to the desk where he had just been seated.

Am I dead?

It felt like his body was rocketing through space, but he had no body. There was no space, no darkness, no stars or planets. There was just vast nothingness.

Then, as quickly as he had been swept away, his body came to a complete stop. It was disorienting, as if he was going from nothing to something, turning instantly from a gas to a solid. The nothingness gave way to a brilliant flash of light. It was blinding it was so bright and hurt his eyes. Then color slowly started appearing as the world slowly came into focus. There were shapes- a four post bed, a dresser, a bookshelf and an empty toy box. Sounds filled his ears, mostly hollering and gunfire. He felt the solid floor beneath him. He also felt the sticky warmness he was sitting in. The world had returned.

Raising his hand he saw it was covered in white fur and dripping crimson wetness. For the first time he realized that the muzzle of the revolver was still in his mouth and he was biting down on it hard enough to crack his two front teeth. He removed it and looked around. It was obvious he was in a little girl's bedroom. What wasn't obvious was what he was sitting in, until he saw the bloody raw nub of the fluffy white cotton tail.

"Peter?" He slowly saw the ravaged shape of Peter Cottontail beneath him.

"Santa? Is it really you?"

Looking up, Santa was instantly startled by the other body in the room. The 632 Smith & Wesson revolver was instinctively leveled at the thing in the room.

"Whoa, big man! Slow down, dude." The thing put its hands up in surrender. "Chill, man. It's cool. Put the piece away."

The only way to describe the creature was to say it was a living doll, a patchwork rag doll the size of a man. Coiled strands of green yarn covered its head. It had two shiny black button eyes and a stitched open slit for a mouth. Colorful purple overalls covered its body, the upper half of which was covered in a long sleeve orange shirt. Its hands were made of oversized white gloves with only three fingers on each hand.

40

It wore shiny black boots on its feet. Santa thought of the raggedy man as being like a scarecrow, only where a scarecrow would have straw poking from the ends of its shirt sleeves and pants cuffs, the doll man had strands of loose cotton stuffing sticking out.

"Seriously, dude, lower the heat. I know this is weird and you're freaked out, but there are explanations. Trust me."

Santa didn't know what to make of the rag doll man. Flesh eating zombies were one thing, but giant sized living dolls were a complete other. Revolver still leveled at the creature, Santa struggled in the Easter Bunny's blood, fur and exposed innards to heft his bulk upright.

"Is this..." He couldn't finish the thought. His boots made squelching, sucking noises as he stepped out of the gory mess. He knew the answer anyway.

"Yeah, damn, the hoppity dude didn't know what hit him. He was scared. They climbed up and got in through the window. There were too many of them."

"There were too many of what?" Santa backed away a couple steps and then noticed the open window. There had been a struggle. The pink curtains were splashed with crimson splotches.

"Are you being serious? Deaders, man. Surely you've noticed all the dead dudes walking around." The raggedy man's tone took a sarcastic bent.

Peter had been torn to shreds by those things. Then something crunched underfoot. Lifting his boot Santa found a pair of bloody dragonfly-like wings stuck to the tread.

"The Tooth Fairy," the rag doll man offered solemnly.

41

"One of the deaders ate her right out of the air, like catching a snowflake. Sick, man." It shook its head.

"Who are you?" Santa asked, still pointing the revolver as menacingly as he could muster. He had never really been known for being much of a bad ass, except maybe to the occasional kid who still got a stocking full of coal. He wasn't even sure if he was holding the revolver properly.

"Binky," the life size doll man said with a spring. "Come on, I'll take you to meet the boss. She's in the big bedroom. I'll lead the way." He offered to let Santa go first, but the big, not-so-jolly man was reluctant to have his back to the doll man, so Binky led the way.

As they walked down the hallway, Santa heard the chaos of war all around him. In one bedroom, a nursery, a battalion of twelve inch G.I. Jeff action dolls of vintage pedigree was at the two windows firing their miniature weapons at the creatures down below. In the next room, a gaggle of Fashion Fancy Francine dolls was pushing Molotov cocktails in Zip Cola bottles over the edge of the window sills after lighting them. Santa heard the bottles crash below with a whoosh, the "deaders" in the near vicinity going up in flames. He could smell their rotting flesh cooking in the swirl of the winter chilled air.

"The boss is working overtime. She's been keeping the deaders at bay all day. If she seems a little grouchy it's because we ran out of the strawberry Toaster Poppers she likes. She can't seem to wish up any more of them. Weird how that works, huh?" Santa had no idea what the doll man was talking about.

"We've been able to get her to eat some cereal and some macaroni and cheese, but, you know, they aren't strawberry Toaster Poppers." The rag doll man stopped at the end of the hallway and opened the door to the master bedroom.

There was a flurry of activity inside the room. Stuffed animals of all kinds, Pandas, sea turtles, giraffes and monkeys, manned the window sills. Each was tossing steak knives and good silver forks like seasoned Big Top Circus knife throwers. Their aim was always on target, blasting into the deaders wandering around the backyard. Some of the dead things were blazing from the Molotov cocktails, but even the fire didn't seem to stop them.

A large teddy bear brought more projectiles, deadly sharpened pencils to be used as arrows for makeshift bows. Like fire wood, the stuffed bear's arms were full and he dropped the pile near a group of Precious Ponies. The living plastic ponies were making bows from rubber bands and Popsicle sticks.

In the center of the ever moving chaos was a seven year old girl. Her blonde hair was long and curly, pulled back in a ponytail. She wore footie pajamas as well as a ballerina's tutu, a cape made from a bath towel secured with a safety pin and a plastic, bejeweled tiara. Standing next to her was a brown haired boy who looked roughly the same age. His shape was faint, like he wasn't really there. He was nearly transparent. Santa recognized both children.

"Make sure them nasty deaders aren't crawling up the side of the house again. Use the pencil arrows to shoot out their eyes. Maybe if they can't see they won't get so close to the house." When Franny Parker saw Santa Claus she stopped completely, eyes wide, mouth open. "You're real! And you're packing heat," she added exuberantly, noticing the Smith & Wesson revolver. "I hope you know how to use that thing."

"Franny Parker? Dalton Chambers?" Santa was confused. Where were little Franny's parents? Why was Dalton Chambers here? The boy hadn't been on the "Good" list since Christmas 1971. It was the fall of '72 when he took sick with pneumonia and...

"Are you listening to me?" The little girl stood with her hands on her hips, the same way her mom talked to her dad when he was supposed to be mowing the grass instead of watching baseball on TV.

"What?" Santa felt very confused. The situation at the North Pole had suddenly gone from nightmare status to fever dream freak-out status.

"I said it's cool that you know my imaginary friend, Dalton, but did you come to save us? Do you have your sleigh and eight tiny reindeer on the roof ready to fly us out of here?"

Santa just stared at the little girl, more confused than before.

"Am I messing up my words or something? Are you not the real Santa? Did I get some old drunk sidewalk Santa, one of them bell ringing ones that stands outside of S-Mart during the shopping season?" Her little hands were still on her hips.

"No, I'm the real Santa." His voice was tiny, so small in the commotion around him. Toys battling the living dead –

deaders - it was too unreal. And he was Santa Claus for crying out loud! He lived at the North Pole. He had flying reindeer and worked with honest to goodness elves and flew around the entire world in one night. But this was too much.

"Good, cause not all of you guys are real." She held up her tiny hand, her little fingers splayed out. "Bigfoot, the Loch Ness Monster, the Bogey Man, Leprechauns and little green men from Mars are not real, not real, not real, not real and not real." She drew in a finger for each one until her little hand was making a fist. "I got the Easter Bunny and the Tooth Fairy, a lot of good they did me. Then we thought of you. So, are you here with your sleigh to fly us away or what?"

"No. I just...*appeared* here. I don't know what happened or how I got here."

"Great. Maybe I ought to have wished for Chuck Norris or some robot ninjas instead." She tapped her foot like she'd seen her mom do when she was trying to solve a problem.

"Where are your parents?"

"Oh, let me tell you, Santa. Them numbskulls ran off and left me. When the deaders attacked the neighborhood, everyone got together to get over to the high school. Well, my parents were so worried about my stupid little baby brother they ran out of here without me. I was asleep in my toy box. I like to pretend it's a fort. Anyway, that old dumb baby's only a couple months old and I've been their daughter for seven whole years and they left me behind. Now I'm just trying to get to them."

"What is all this?" Frustrated, Santa shook his hands in the air around the buzz of activity. "How did your toys come to life?"

"I don't know. I just wished them to come to life. Actually, I just started making wishes. Some stuff comes true and some stuff doesn't. I guess there're rules or something."

"Why don't you just wish yourself to safety with your family?"

The little girl rolled her eyes. "I already thought of that, Santee. It don't work. I wished them here and that don't work either. I've seen some of the neighbors try to make it to the house to get me, but every time they try they get attacked. I wish them back so they don't get hurt. These dumb wishes won't just let me wish myself out of here or my family back here. I can't even wish for any more Toaster Poppers." A slight look of disgust washed over her then was gone.

"So all of this..." he waved his hands around again, motioning to the living toys.

"This is my army. The first thing I did was wish my imaginary friends Binky and Dalton to life. Binky's that rag doll. I draw pictures of him all the time. He looks exactly how I like to draw him. He should be a toy. I think everyone would like to play with him. Dalton didn't change any. He's still like a shadow, just hangs around. He can't pick anything up, but he helps out with ideas and stuff, like wishing you here. That was his idea."

The little boy looked solemnly from where he stood in the room. His image shimmied, like a heat wave off the desert. Behind him, the ponies fired sharpened pencils from the open second story windows into the eyes of the undead below.

"Why don't you just wish for a helicopter," Santa said.

His mind still could not comprehend a child who could make wishes come true.

"You know how to fly a helicopter, Santee?" The jolly old elf just looked at her with a blank expression. "Well, me neither."

"These toys aren't going to hold those things off forever," Santa said. For the first time little Franny looked worried. The little girl had been on her own since her parents left her behind and she had been resourceful enough to hold back the living dead until now. She had been granted a wonderful gift that could mean their salvation if she could figure out how to use it properly. She looked frustrated.

"I gotta go think about stuff," she said finally, storming out of her parent's room, on the verge of tears. She went to the hallway bathroom and slammed the door behind her. She'd heard her dad say time and time again the bathroom was where he did his best thinking.

Santa moved out of the way as more toys brought in household items to be used as weapons against the undead. He marveled at how they worked together. He looked over at the boy.

"Does she know?"

Dalton shook his head. "She thinks I'm an imaginary friend. She saw me for the first time two years ago. Not only can she see me, we can talk. It freaks her parents out. They just say it's her imagination, but sometimes they talk, and they suspect I'm more than that. But as far as she's concerned, I'm just a figment of her imagination."

"What happened?" Santa remembered the Christmas

47

he brought Dalton a shiny blue bicycle. He remembered every present he ever delivered to every boy and girl in the world. The boy had been so excited that Christmas morning. Unfortunately, it had been his last.

"I got lost, Santa. My Grandma and Grandpa came for me, but I wanted to stay with my parents. Grandma Red was calling for me, but I didn't go to her, and then the light just faded away. I stayed here with my parents, but then they moved away. They couldn't live here any longer. I got stuck here and I haven't seen them since they left. I don't even know if they're still alive. I've been so lonely, until Franny came to live here. Now I have a friend."

Santa felt his heart breaking for this poor little boy. Trapped between two worlds, all he wanted to do was get back to his family.

Little Franny returned, a glint of determination sparkling in her eyes. "I know what I'm gonna wish for. I saw a movie and I think this fella can help us."

"What are you doing?" Santa looked concerned.

Eyes closed, little hands balled into tight fists, at the top of her voice she screeched, "I wish for King Kong!"

One eye popped opened and looked around and then the other. She tilted her head a little to listen. All she could here were the moaning and groaning of the undead outside and the steady whoosh of the Molotov cocktails.

"Nothing?" she asked in a quiet voice. Dalton just shook his head. "Dang it! That old stupid monkey ain't even real. Back to the drawin' board, I guess."

"Can you wish to go back into time, like maybe to

before all this happened?" Santa suggested.

"Already tried, big man. Look, you gotta figure, I done tried all the good wishes before I had to stoop to wishing for the Easter Bunny and the Tooth Fairy. I mean, really. I'm out of ideas."

"How about..." Santa was cut off by screaming coming from behind him. The ponies were neighing frantically. Suddenly, a dead, rotten hand reached over the window sill as a deader climbed into the room. Another was close behind.

"Shoot it, Santa!" Franny cried.

Raising the revolver Santa fired two shots. Both hit the deader in the forehead. The force of the blast knocked it loose of the window frame, but the next creature crawled in right after it.

"Dudes! The deaders are in the house!" Binky screamed as he came running into the master bedroom. The stink of the undead filled the house. Franny's dad's collection of G.I. Jeff soldiers were cutting a hasty retreat, still firing as the living dead poured in from every door and window on the first story of the house.

"Think of something," Santa shouted as he blasted the second zombie climbing into the room. This one had pencils sticking from each eye. It was blind, but it still found its way inside.

"I don't know," the little girl cried. Tears started streaming from her big hazel colored eyes. "I just want my mommy and daddy. I wish they were here." Nothing happened. Louder she screamed, "I wish my mommy and daddy were here!"

"There's too many of them, man!" Binky exclaimed excitedly, waving his arms around wildly, stray wads of stuffing flying every which way.

"We've got to do something," Santa said. He fired the last of the slugs into the dead things coming down the hallway.

"I wish for a magic wand!" Franny screamed.

In a puff of smoke and a boom of thunder a black wand eighteen inches in length with a golden tip appeared before her feet. She snapped it up and swung it around.

"What does it do?" Santa asked. After emptying the revolver he threw it at the closest monster entering the bedroom. It bounced of the deader's head and slid under the bed.

"Watch this." The little girl ran to the nearest deader. The creature looked down at her like it was a starving dog and she was a tasty fried pork chop. Snarling, baring its teeth, the deader moved in to snatch her.

"You're a jack in the box!" With that she poked the undead creature with the golden point of the wand. There was a puff of smoke and when it cleared a smiley faced clown on a spring swayed back and forth in a musical box. Franny's smile went ear to ear.

"Look out!" Santa said, pointing towards the door. A horde of the dead things were rushing into the room.

Moving fast she ran from one creature to the other, hitting each one with the wand after saying what they were to become. "You're a football! You're a Frisbee! You're a Beach Blanket Fashion Francine Doll! You're a coloring book! And you're a Binky doll!" She moved through the horde and when she was done the hallway was littered with brand new toys.

"You've done it!" Santa exclaimed. "Now wish for some more wands so we can get out of here."

Wishing wands for Santa and Binky, the trio made their way outside. By the time they moved through the crowd of deaders, the streets were scattered with piles of new toys. They met up with others hiding in the shadows and made their way across town. At the high school, re-united with her parents, Franny wished for magic wands for everyone and showed them how to use them. Soon, the town had piles of new toys from one end to the other. There was not an undead creature in sight.

"I wish for a new sleigh and eight new tiny reindeer." There was a puff of smoke and a crack of thunder and the new sleigh and reindeer appeared.

"Put the wands into the magic toy bags," Santa told everyone. "I won't run out until I give the last one away." Their town was safe. Now he had to distribute the wands around the world.

"Can I go with you?" Franny asked hopefully.

"You certainly may," Santa said with a wink.

"I don't know," her mother started, then the baby began crying and she had to tend to him. Franny's father gave her a "thumbs up" and she hopped into the front of the sleigh with Santa. She was still wearing the tutu, cape and tiara with her footie pajamas. Binky climbed in next her.

As they started into the air, little Franny exclaimed, "I hope everyone has at least one wish that comes true tonight!"

Then they were gone.

Unseen by anyone except for Franny and Santa Claus, a beam of light shot through the night sky and circled on a little boy, her imaginary friend Dalton. Dalton smiled brightly as his Grandma Red came to him, engulfing him in her big warm arms, embracing her grandson. His Grandpa was there too, and his parents. They were all as he remembered them. His wish had finally come true. Dalton was at last reunited with his family.

Over the course of one night, Santa, Franny and Binky delivered magic wands to every corner of the world. Franny wished that people would know how to use them as soon as they gave them the wands. It only took a short time before those holed up fending off the living dead were turning the hideous, blood thirsty creatures into harmless toys.

By early morning, the threat of the deaders was over. The world was covered with people tending to their wounds and piles of brand new toys, many of them Binky dolls, which were suddenly all the rage that Christmas. It was a different world, as people had banded together and all worked for a united cause. It was a good world.

As the sun started waking up the land, Santa flew overhead to return little Franny to her parents. With a smile as dazzling as the morning sun she exclaimed excitedly, "I wish everyone a Merry Christmas and a Happy New Year!"

IT CAME UPON A MIDNIGHT CLEAR
BY THOMAS M. MALAFARINA

"It matters little," she said, softly. "To you, very little. Another idol has displaced me; and if it can cheer and comfort you in time to come, as I would have tried to do, I have no just cause to grieve." - A Christmas Carol, Charles Dickens

The solitary car moved slowly along the empty main street of town. The man behind the wheel was not paying attention to the darkened storefronts or the emptiness of the thoroughfare. It was after 11:30 PM and although he was heading home, his mind was still back at the office where it always seemed to be, obsessed with issues, which should have been resolved long before he left. Then again, there were always issues needing resolution and he knew even if he worked twenty-four hours a day, seven days a week he still would never be able to take care of all of them. It seemed for every single problem he managed to rectify three more came forward to take their place.

The night was clear and every star could be seen for miles in the cloudless Pennsylvania sky. The temperature was surprisingly mild for December twenty-fourth, Christmas Eve. For those local residents hoping for a white Christmas, the pleasant temperatures would likely prove disappointing. But the man took no notice to the beautiful night or the pleasant weather.

Fifty-six year old Evan Flint had no need for Christmas, no desire to celebrate the holiday or, for that matter, no one to share it with had he chosen to do so. At first glance, one might think he had everything a man could want out of life, his being the richest man in the county if not the state. If one were to ask him, Evan would likely agree, stating categorically that he had absolutely no need for a wife, children, friends or other such things he often referred to as the trappings of life; he had more money than he could spend in three lifetimes and his fortune continued to grow daily. But he would be wrong.

He was the sole owner of a manufacturing company located on the outskirts of a small Schuylkill County town. The factory employed well over two thousand residents from all over the county. It was one of the few remaining manufacturing facilities where one could at least attempt to earn a living. For most of the workers it felt more like a prison and for many it was. Those residents who had overextended their credit or had lost what few savings they had during the downturn in the economy had little choice but to tolerate the meager pay and substandard working conditions offered at Flint Manufacturing.

The benefits Evan offered were equally substandard but he knew about his workers pitiful financial situations and had no qualms about taking advantage of each and every one of them. He realized if the economy were good he would likely lose most of the better workers who would leave to seek employment elsewhere, but with the economy in the drink he could do with them as he pleased. To say the least, very few of his workers were happy.

He was aware of the various derogatory nicknames they called him behind his back such as Evan-eezer or Skin Flint; all pertaining to his being a tightwad. When he first heard of the nicknames, Evan had fired a hand full of workers who he had determined started the whole mess, thanks to a few of his loyal cronies who brought him all the news. However, as is always true of such monikers, once they were spoken aloud, they seemed to stick. And soon it became apparent to Evan that he would either have to learn to ignore the snide remarks or fire his entire workforce.

The particular name, which seemed to bother him the most, was Evan-eezer, as it was a play on the character Ebenezer Scrooge from Charles Dickens' classic "A Christmas Carol". This name really irked him the most because it summed up the complete ingratitude his workforce felt toward him. After all he had managed to keep them all employed hadn't he?

Although he thought of himself as conservative, thrifty and careful with his finances, he did not like being lumped in with that miserly character. At least he did not think of himself as such a man. However, if he took the time to consider the possibility, Evan would soon discover his own life actually had many parallels with the fictitious Scrooge's.

Like Scrooge, Evan was a loner as a child with few if any friends. As a young man in college, he had met, fallen in love with and married a beautiful young woman whose name was Claire. Scrooge has he own love during his early years.

Within a year of their getting married, Evan had started

his manufacturing company as a partnership with a young man named Jack Worley. Scrooge had started his company with his partner Jacob Marley. Scrooge's partner died, leaving him to run the business alone. A similar thing happened to Evan's partner Jack.

Whereas Evan had come from nothing and worked long hours and most weekends to build the business, his partner Jack came from old money and was known throughout the area as a reckless playboy. Though it was true Jack had put up the initial startup money for the company, he had no real interest in the business itself and gladly left the running of the day-to-day affairs to Evan. But his shiftless behavior nonetheless irritated Evan to the point of near insanity.

Evan's marriage ended after just a few short years, when Claire tired of the long hours he spent at work. Evan explained that he was only working so hard to build a future for the two of them, but she did not seem to care. She had no need for money, or the finer things of life. She simply wanted the man she married to be there for her and he could not be. On the day she left, Claire told him his true love was not really her, but money and power. This was another parallel to Scrooge and his own lost love.

After Claire left, Evan immersed himself further in his work, having nothing else to fill his empty hours. Within a few years, he had single handedly built the manufacturing company to a booming business employing over one thousand people. While other companies were closing and sending their products overseas to be made, Evan was growing and expanding and continuing to hire more workers weekly.

All he while Evan was working, Jack did little to contribute to the business, but continued to take his share of the profits. Evan knew this kind of behavior had to end, and he had to find a way to stop him. Then one day Jack was killed in a tragic boating accident. The man had been at the New Jersey shore having a private party on his favorite boat with several young coeds when a freak explosion killed him and all of his passengers. For a while, Evan Flint was considered a person of interest in the disaster.

When questioned by authorities, Evan didn't even bother to feign the slightest remorse at the loss of his partner. He even stated that as far as he was concerned, it was some sort of cosmic divine intervention. Then police discovered when the pair had started the company, both Evan and Jack took out substantial life insurance policies, each naming the other as sole beneficiary. This fact, along with his less then mournful attitude toward his partner's death, was why Evan came under scrutiny.

The policy Jack had taken was worth well over five million dollars, all of which went to Evan. Needless to say, the police felt this alone was motive enough for his wanting his partner dead. However, following a thorough police investigation, it was determined to have simply been an unavoidable freak accident and Evan was exonerated of all suspicion.

But the townspeople and the workers at his factory were never completely satisfied with the authorities' findings.

For as much as they disliked Evan with his sullen, much too serious disposition, they all seemed to love Jack with is wild and outwardly friendly personality. Evan was quite certain if they had a choice, each one of the townspeople, most of whom were also his employees, would have preferred if he had died instead.

Evan felt his workers were ungrateful and unappreciative of him and all he had done for them. The world was currently going through one of the worst economic recessions since the great depression and millions of people were unemployed with no chance of finding a decent job. This was true in the areas of the country were jobs were generally plentiful. But in his area of Pennsylvania, even during times of economic prosperity, jobs were always hard to find.

On many occasions, he had fought back attempts to bring in labor unions many times and had always been successful. But he was concerned that his latest planned changed in company benefits might push his workforce too far. He had some underlying discomfort that perhaps his next move might be the proverbial straw that broke the camel's back.

One benefit his workers still enjoyed which most companies had abandoned years earlier was a pension plan. But now Evan had decided he would have to take drastic measures to keep his company competitive with the offshore manufacturers and keep his own personal fortune growing as well. The result was that he had decided to do away with the company pension plan. He would essentially freeze the pension, so no one would lose any time and benefits they had accrued to date, but he would not support any additional increase in the plan. From March or April of the next year on, he would institute a 401K savings plan where employees could put in their own money to save to take care of their own retirement.

Both Evan's company controller and vice president of manufacturing tried to change his mind about the move, complaining that not only would it hurt employee morale but it might also cause a mass exodus of workers from the company. Evan knew that although they might gripe and complain as usual, there was no way they would consider walking out in this hostile economic climate. Perhaps in a few years, if the economy started to recover they might think about it but by then the initial pain would be long forgotten. Besides, he was also confident that any company that would hire them would not have a pension plan either.

The reason Evan was feeling stressed now on his drive home was likely because of the very argument he had with his two top executives earlier in the day. "Screw 'em all!" He thought to himself. "They can all go pound sand as far as I am concerned. I am the Chief Executive Officer of this company and my word is gospel. I am the only one looking out for their futures. They are the sheep and I am the shepherd. I founded this company; that makes me the creator, which means I am God as far as they are all concerned. And if I say this is how things have to be, then so be it."

All of his workers were off for one day for the Christmas holiday but would be returning to work in the day after Christmas. A large number of them saved vacation for the time between Christmas and New Year's Day but most would be back at work. He planned to make the announcement through his communication channels first thing the start of the next business day. He chuckled to himself thinking about what a terrible Christmas present they would all be receiving.

Soon Evan had passed through town and was on a rural road heading out into the country to his estate. He turned into his driveway and paused in front of the eight foot ornately decorated iron gates blocking his access. Pressing a button on his remote control unit the gates swung invitingly open and he continued up his long driveway, the gates closing automatically behind him. As Evan approached the front of his luxurious three-story brick mansion, he pressed another button and watched the first of four huge bay doors of his garage open.

Closing the garage door behind him, Evan entered the kitchen area of his home and quickly typed in his security code to suppress the shrill scream of the alarm system. The house was suddenly thrust into silence, blessed silence.

Evan walked into the living room and pressed a button on a control console illuminating a reading light behind a large leather chair across the room. He glanced across the room at the tall grandfather clock he had purchased from a clockmaker in Switzerland; the time was now 11:50 pm.

Then with the press of another button the large gas fireplace burst into flames, washing the room with its glow and comforting warmth. Evan walked over to a bar next to the fireplace and poured himself a large glass of whiskey over ice.

He sat down on the chair, allowing himself to sink deeply into the upholstery. After a few long gulps of his nightcap, his mind began to wander back to a much happier time, back to when he and Claire had been married and in love. Back then he always looked forward to coming home from work and finding her there.

During those years they had no money and lived in a small apartment above a pharmacy on the main street. He always promised Claire someday they would have more money than she could imagine, but she never seemed to care. And on the day she left, he finally understood, much too late that she did not want things but wanted him.

He heard she had remarried a few years later and the last he knew, she was living in another state. She apparently had four grown children and a herd of grandchildren. He supposed she was happy in her new life but he truly no longer thought much about her, except at times like this. He had his company and his money and he insisted that was all he needed out of life. But sometimes he felt so very bitter over the loss of his wife.

Not wanting to dwell on the painful memories of his past, he took a few more generous swigs of his drink, grabbed the TV remote control for the sixty-inch flat screen mounted above the mahogany fireplace mantel and turned it on. He mindlessly surfed from channel to channel, perhaps hoping for something to stir his interest.

After a while, he stopped at a channel, which was playing the 1938 classic black and white film adaptation of Charles Dickens' "A Christmas Carol". The scene currently displayed on the screen depicted Jacob Marley's ghost howling and rattling his chains madly as only one suffering the tortures of an eternity in hell could do.

"Bah Humbug!" Evan said, chuckling to himself, enjoying the way he was lampooning the Christmas classic and already feeling the effects of the whiskey. He pressed the off button on the TV remote and the giant screen went black. He sat quietly in his large chair and finished his drink. After a moment, he got to his feet and discovered he was surprisingly off kilter. He had not expected to become so drunk so quickly but thinking back, he realized he had not eaten since breakfast. No wonder he was half hammered. Suddenly he was startled by the sound of the grandfather clock striking midnight. "Time for bed." He said to the empty room

As he was regaining his balance and attempting to stagger out toward the hallway, he heard a strange noise coming from the foyer, near the front door. It was then he realized he had disarmed the security system to get in but never rearmed it. He began to wonder if some low-life scum from town had taken it upon himself to attempt a robbery on this Christmas Eve. If so, Evan was prepared to give the criminal a present he had never anticipated. He walked over to the fireplace and clumsily withdrew a large rod-iron poker with a menacing looking tip. Holding the doorframe for support, he slowly peered around the corner to look out toward the front door.

What he saw caught him completely by surprise. There was no would-be burglar skulking inside the door, in fact the entire hallway was empty; at least he initially thought it was empty. Then Evan noticed something strange. It was as if the air in the hall close to the door was changing its physical structure. It seemed at first to shimmer then to ripple in almost liquidy waves. Then a shape started to form within the distorted air.

It appeared to be some sort of mass, low to the floor, perhaps only two feet high at its apex in the center then tapering downward on sides forming an elliptical series of pulsating and bubbling lumps. At first, it reminded Evan of an enormous fried egg with a large flesh-colored dome in the center tapering down on the sides. In fact the entire thing seemed to be flesh-like not only in color but in its appearance. It was in constant motion, undulating and bubbling wildly. After a few moments, the waves of air stopped and the thing in the hall seemed to solidify and become real.

"What the hell!" Evan exclaimed in shock raising the poker high above his head, prepared to lash out at the strange living nightmare just a few feet in front of him. Suddenly the pulsating shape began to move toward him under some form of propulsion he could not begin to understand. As it got closer, Evan could see large spidery veins, some as thick as rope, pulsating throughout its hideous form. It was then he noticed a disgustingly foul stench emanating from the strange being. It made his stomach turn with revulsion, the thing smelling like a long-dead rotting corpse.

At first he took a cautious step away from the vile creature then driven either by a courage brought on by the whiskey or else plain and simple stupidity, he decided to lunge forward with the poker and attempt to attack the thing.

63

He plunged the sharp end of the poker deep into the front side of the mass, close to the large center dome. He let go of the handle out of sheer disgust upon feeling the unearthly consistency of the thing. The poker seemed to sink harmlessly into the throbbing glob of vein-riddled flesh then spring back out and fall to the floor.

Evan was suddenly hit with an incredible pain in the center of his own gut, which doubled him over for a moment, before it began to slowly subside and he could once again stand semi-erect. It was as if he were feeling the pain, which he had meant to inflict on the thing.

He staggered backward a step or two and wondered aloud "What manner of creature is this ungodly thing." He started to turn to run for the back door when suddenly he heard a soft liquidy voice hissing behind him, "Where... do you think... you are going?"

He stopped in his tracks and turned around slowly; convinced the hideous twitching blob on his hallway floor had just impossibly spoken to him. "Wha…what?" He stammered.

"No need to run Evan...That's right...I know who you are...as I should." The thing seemed to say to him, although he could not quite make out any mechanism by which the creature had articulated the words. Then he thought he noticed a long slit forming in the center of the dome, running vertically rather than horizontally. It opened slightly and the stench he had originally smelled became even more pungent.

Then he saw the slit begin to vibrate as he heard the voice once again. "So...Evan...What special plans do you have for this Christmas Eve?...Where are the friends?...Where is the merriment?...Where is the celebration?"

Evan was confused beyond comprehension. He shouted angrily at the pulsating gelatinous mass. "Who the hell are you? What manner of being are you? And why are you here?"

Once again the long slit began to vibrate, resembling the wave of an oscilloscope and the foul odor and voice appeared once again. "Why Evan, don't you recognize me?"

"What in the name of God are you talking about?" Evan shouted. "How could I recognize you? You are more revolting than the creatures of my worst nightmares? Recognize you? I don't even know what you are?"

The blob-like mass slid with stealth toward Evan. He was too preoccupied and confused to notice and as a result did not step back. The creature spoke in a calm and almost hypnotic voice. "Tonight is Christmas Eve...You should be spending it with your loved ones...Not sitting here in the dark, in this prison you call a home...But then again, you have no loved ones do you Evan?"

Now Evan was becoming angered to the extent that his initial fear and disgust had fled, replaced by his natural defensive nature. "What do you know of me? Nothing! You are just some hallucination, the result of too little food and too much drink. Hell, tomorrow morning I probably won't remember any of this. Be gone you revolting apparition."

"On the contrary," the thing corrected, "I will not be going anywhere...You know that Christmas Eve is a time for miracles...After tonight, things will never be the same for you again...Look closer Evan...Isn't there anything about me

65

which seems familiar to you?"

Evan stared at the disgusting slimy rippling mass of veins and flesh and knew he had never seen anything like it before. Yet, somehow there really was something about the creature which he actually did seem to recognize. It was not something he could see but something intangible which he seemed to feel; something almost telepathic.

"Ah!" The mass said through its rippling slit of a mouth. "There is some recognition after all…Do you care to venture a guess about my origin, Evan?…Do you have the nerve to try?" The creature slid even closer to the unsuspecting man.

Then suddenly the realization hit Evan like a ton of bricks and he understood everything. "You --- are you saying --- you are *me*?"

"That's right Evan." The blob said. "I am the physical manifestation of your immortal soul…I am you Evan…This is what you have become inside…A vile, disgusting mass of anger, hatred and bitterness…No love or kindness or beauty exists in me because such human traits no longer exist in you…You have become a living disease; a blight on the face of the earth…All you care about is yourself and your money…Clair was right Evan…She had to leave you because you only have one love in your life…Your insatiable greed."

"It can't be!" Evan screamed, "You're can't be me! You're nothing like me! You are just some figment born of whiskey! Leave my house now!" He made a drunken, futile gesture, pointing his hand towards the front door. It was then that he realized the massive globule was just inches away from him.

He tried to back away, but before he could make a single step backward a long, thin ropelike tongue shot out from the mouth slit and wrapped itself tightly around Evan's neck. It burned the flesh on his neck and Evan could feel his breath being cut off by the fleshy lasso. Then the ropy tongue began to retract into the creature as the slit of a mouth grew in size from just a few inches to more than a foot and a half in length.

As Evan was pulled, screaming as best as his lack of air would permit, toward the slit the sides separated and opened to reveal a giant black opening. At the base of the slit a stream of blood-red black liquid slowly dripped out and down along the creature's still pulsating flesh.

Evan's head was soon inside the thing's mouth, which closed tightly around his shoulders. Soon Evan's cries became muffled and then were silenced. The sides of the slit began to ripple even more frantically, slowly working the rest of Evan's twitching body further inside. His body thrashed and flayed as it was sucked deeper into the beast. Within a few short moments, any traces that Evan Flint ever existed were completely gone.

The creature remained in the hallway for a few more moments, as if making sure it's job was finished. Then it slowly began to fade until it was completely gone, along with the man whose greed had made its temporary existence possible on this clear Christmas Eve.

SEVEN DAYS UNTIL CHRISTMAS
BY BRANDON CRACRAFT

Mario chewed off his fingernails, spat them into a trashcan beside his desk, then bit into his fingertips. I still didn't know how Mario Alvarez got a management position. He hated any kind of responsibility.

"Hate to do this to you, Billy," he finally said, shuffling through the official paperwork. "I just want you to know that it isn't my idea." He held his breath for a few seconds, then started pounding on the dented metal desk and let out a string of curses in English and Spanish. "I got to fire you, buddy. I don't have a choice."

I went pale. I never expected him to say that. He knew I didn't do it. I figured that the worst he would give me was a write up. "You know that Jack stole the money from the register. You know that he's a meth head. He smells like one. First ten dollars comes up missing from Barb's register and now---"

"If your register is missing more than twenty dollars," he said slowly, "you are fired." My grey eyes bored into him, remembering a time when we all emptied our pockets so that his register would only be short eighteen dollars and change one evening. "I don't think you stole the money, even given your past."

Anger burned under my skin and tied my intestines in

knots. I could see Mario's weed hanging out of his front pocket, and I was pretty sure that he didn't have a prescription for it. It didn't matter what I said. Jack was dealing for half of the people who worked at the taco stand.

I reached into my wallet and Mario ducked. I took out counted out forty dollars in fives and singles. "It's all I got, but you can have it if you let me stay. Tell the boss that you found it stuck in my register." My eyebrows narrowed. "Kind of like we did when you lost that money, because you were too busy checking out the ass on those high school girls."

"Dude, I told you not to bring that up," he said, suddenly angry. "Look, there's nothing I can do about it. When the owner found out about the missing register, he told me that I had to fire you." He looked away, a sign that he was lying. "I told him that you were a great employee and had been working here eight months now."

I shook my head. "It'll be one year next week." I bit my lip, surprised that my temper remained buried in my chest. I guess the pills were working after all. "Can't I just work until the end of this paycheck? I'll have enough for rent. You can't just leave me hanging like this. Think of how many times I've covered for you."

Mario let out a loud sigh and started talking to me like I was a kid. I hated when people did that. I was twenty-eight years old. "Think of it this way, Billy. You wanted some time off to spend with your kid. Didn't you say something about finally getting to see him this Christmas?"

Something inside me burst and I slammed my fist against the desk before I realized that I moved and had my face less than an inch away from Mario's pock marked nose. "I haven't seen my son for three years. Three fucking years. Can you imagine that? No. I know you have bastards all over this city and probably every disease of the dick known to man. This was my chance to finally see my son. I finally convinced Sylvia and the courts that I was responsible enough to spend Christmas with my son. Do you think they'll let me see him if I don't have a place to live. That was one of the conditions of me seeing Racer. I had to prove to them that I could keep a job and a place to live."

Mario gnawed on his thumb and avoided eye contact. "That's not my problem, Billy."

"What am I supposed to do? I can't just move back in with my Grandma. Sylvia would make sure that I never saw Racer again."

Mario started to look scared and swallowed audibly. "That's not my problem, Billy. I don't think you stole the money, but maybe you made a mistake. You've had an attitude on you lately."

"Have any of the customers complained?" I asked him point blank. "I'm always friendly and cheerful with them. A lot of them tell me that they look forward to seeing me here."

"None of the customers," Mario admitted. "You know that a lot of us hang out and hit the bars and stuff after work. You never hang out. Jack saw you with that cop the other day. We're kind of afraid that you're a Narc. Not everyone here is legal, you know. Rosalita---"

"That's my best friend," I told him. "He's just a traffic cop. He doesn't have anything to do with border patrol." I tasted bile and blood. "Besides, you're not worried that I'm going to turn Rosalita into immigration. You think I'm going to let Grady know how many of you are still using."

It was Mario's turn to slam the desk, hitting it repeatedly like a toddler having a tantrum. "I've done all I can for you. I'm sure that you can get your cop friend or someone to help you out. I don't care about your kid, and I'm sick of your holier than thou attitude just because you knocked up some cougar when you were still in high school. We all screwed Sylvia. You ain't special, Billy."

"Shut up!" I yelled as I kicked the door open and stomped out through the taco stand. I used every curse word that I could think, trying to stay angry so Mario, Jack, and the others wouldn't see me cry. Once I got into the parking lot, I turned back one last time to flip everyone off.

Halfway to my trailer court, I broke down crying. I put up with so much crap from that job, but it didn't matter. I was doing it for Racer, owed it to him. I was a crappy dad, because I was still a stupid kid. Having a baby didn't suddenly grant me powers of maturity and responsibility. I wasn't a little kid anymore. Honestly, neither was he. He was thirteen years old, only year younger than I was when I lost my virginity to town slut Sylvia Markinski.

I shuttered at the thought of my kid being raised without a father. Sylvia Markinski had her own list of problems. From what I hear, he ended up staying with her mother while she was rehab. I had to figure out a way to make a two hundred dollar check stretch into four hundred dollars of rent. If I just could make rent, I could be a part of my son's life...even if it was only visitation every Christmas.

"I'm screwed," I said, before collapsing into self-pity and sobs.

***

Nothing felt more humiliating than looking for a job. The few places that could look past my arrest record crossed my name of the hire list when they realized that I had been fired from my last job. I let my utility bills get pink, hoping that I could scrounge together enough money for rent by selling my clothes and managing to get a couple days of day labor. When I went to the plasma center, they told me that they weren't interested in the blood of a former bisexual drug addict, even though I was never really addicted to weed. I almost exploded on the nurse when I saw her poke holes into a guy whose teeth were yellowed and brittle from meth who lied during the screening process.

When Grady came by with a couple of beers, I knew it was more bad news. I stopped drinking anything but beer, and I saved that for occasions when my life really went to shit. Despite what a lot of folks said, I was never an alcoholic. Alcoholics beat their kids or get behind the wheel drunk. I never did anything. My kidneys just didn't take very kindly to alcohol, and I was about twenty years past the date when wetting the bed meant "accidents" and started getting diagnosed as a "symptom of serious mental illness."

"I talked to your parole officer today, Billy," Grady said, leaning back onto my olive green couch and taking a long pull on his bottle. "Tried to get some help for you, explained the situation."

"Just give me the bad news," I said, staring at the bottle and wondering if I should down it all at once. I set it aside, deciding to give the stomach and kids a break for now. "They can't help me get a job."

"Worse that than," he said. "They want to put you in a halfway house again." He stood up and did his impression of my parole officer, sticking out imaginary tits and pretending to file her nails while looking vapid. "I just don't know if William Nederman is ready to be on his own. He had a difficult time finding a job and he just got fired from this one. How do you get fired from a fast food job, unless you've done something pretty bad?"

I called my parole officer the kind of names I normally reserved for Sylvia. "So I'm screwed. I'll never see Racer again."

Grady gave me a smile. I stood half a foot taller than him, but he outweighed by about fifty pounds of muscle. I always felt like skin and bones next to him. He was the latest of a long line of married, straight men that I had a crush for. Grady was a picture perfect Irish cop: red hair, freckles, crooked, boyish smile. "Do you think I would ever give you bad news without good news?"

Despite all my stress, the hint of smile curled on my lips. I brushed my blond hair out of my eyes and leaned forward. "You managed to talk her out of it?"

"It's actually two part good news," Grady continued. "The first is that I didn't talk her out of the halfway house, just to put all plans to put you back in one of those places away if you can make rent."

"I'll never---"

Grady shook his head, but he was still grinning. "I know how you can make five hundred dollars cash in just twelve days, all tax free. Green backs in your hand for less than one week's work."

I look at him sideways. "I know a lot of ways that I can make that kind of money in just a day, but none of it is legal."

"Billy, I told you that Denise and I were splitting up." I nodded, even though I had never heard an official announcement of their divorce. "She hired Satan as her lawyer, so I'm pretty sure that the bitch is going to take half of my paycheck as child support that my boys will never see." I let out a quick, angry laugh. "Oh, I'm sure that Liam and Pete will see the money as Mommy drives a new car or spends hundreds of dollars on makeup."

"Sorry to hear," I said.

"But I found this," he said, the excitement returning to his voice. He handed me an article about a psychological experiment. It was called the "Seven Days Until Christmas" and required that the participants stay seven days overnight. Not only did it pay five hundred dollars, but all meals were provided. "The bitch can't touch this money, and she already agreed that I can have the boys this Christmas. She wants to go on some vacation to 'discover herself' on my money. I get this five hundred dollars and I spoil the hell of the boys. They've been whining about that new game system."

"I wish I could afford something like that for Racer."

Grady pointed at the five hundred dollars. "Not only will this give you enough money to pay the bills, but you should have enough money to buy Racer the best present. I know it doesn't seem like an awful lot of money, but it's also a week when you don't have to worry about food."

"I guess it could be different," I said hesitantly. "I certainly don't have any better ideas."

Grady held out a beer bottle as a toast. "To our boys and being a Christmastime Daddy. May they get the kind of holiday that they deserve, one that lets them realize just how much we love them." When he put it like that, I didn't know why I hesitated.

***

Professor Elliot Winters looked like Santa Claus with his oversized belly, ruddy complexion, and long white hair and beard. He wore a red shirt and green tie under his lab coat. I never understood the "bowl full of jelly" line until I saw Professor Winters laugh.

"You boys must be William and Philip." He nodded before we had a chance to answer. "You are both fathers to young boys? Mr. Grady, your sons are ten and eight, with your youngest having a ninth birthday in less than a month. Mr. Nederman your son is actually thirteen." He shook his head disapprovingly. "Very young to become a father. Fifteen years old when your son was born and only fourteen when he was conceived. I have to say that you two sound perfect. Should I tell you a little about the experiment?" He pulled out a clipboard and scratched some notes hastily down. When he was done, he leaned closer to us.

"I should say something first," Grady began nervously. "I don't like to be called Philip. People just call me by last name, Grady. I guess it goes back to my time in the Marines and then on the force." He hooked a thumb toward me. "He likes to be called Billy."

"I've been thinking of having it legally changed," I added. "My father's name was William."

Winters smiled, revealing surprisingly yellow teeth. "Do you have issues with your father, Billy?"

I tried to shrug it off. "A few, I guess. Nothing too big."

"Are either of you familiar with my work gentlemen?" Once again, he didn't wait for us to answer. "I have written several textbooks on childhood behavior. I believe in the importance of practical study. I need one week of uninterrupted study on behavior patterns. There will be use of the cell phones and internet. If you decide to leave early, the experiment is considered to be contaminated and you will not be paid."

Grady looked at me and asked the question that was on both of our minds. "How can we help you with a study on childhood behavior?"

"I plan on simulating the childhood experience for the two of you and our other subjects. If you are willing to accept the terms, you will spend the next six and a half days living as children."

"You're not up to anything kinky, are you?" I asked.

Winters let out a hearty laugh, and I thought he was going to fall off his chair. "Nothing so dramatic. I am just trying to determine if it is unhealthy for children to believe in Santa Claus."

"I still don't understand," Grady said. "Billy and I are

both a bit long in the tooth to believe in Santa. I stopped believing in him when I was ten years old. My boys told me there was no Santa Claus on their third day of kindergarten."

Winters nodded. "That does tend to happen earlier and earlier these years. I think it is a shame. Hopefully, you two boys can help prove that point."

"I never told Racer that there was a Santa Claus," I said. "His mother said that it was lying to him."

Winters raised a bushy, white eyebrow. "Did you believe in Santa Claus when you were a little boy, Billy?"

"Yes, sir," I replied, "until I was eight."

"That's excellent, Billy. For the next seven days, you will have all the rights and responsibilities of an eight year old boy. We will simulate you being that age, by removing outside stimulus and having everyone treat you as if you are that age. You will be surprised how easily you will fall into the mindset. You will have a bedtime, chores, all the things associated with being that age. Would you be all right with that arrangement?"

I thought about Racer and nodded my head. "Has to be better than being stuck at a halfway house for God knows how long."

Winters gave me a smile, before turning his attention to Grady. "You said that you sons started disbelieving in Santa Claus when they were in kindergarten. I guess you should be the little brother at five years old."

"I don't understand," Grady said.

Winters looked at Grady and like he really was just a little kid saying things randomly. "It will all makes sense soon, Grady. Don't worry. The most important thing for you to remember is that there really is a Santa Claus." He gave us a knowing wink. "Do you know how I know there is a Santa Claus? Because if you believe in him and you are a good boy, he will give you an extra five hundred dollars. Did you hear that, boys? If you are good boys, you get a thousand dollars."

All doubt about the project wiped away from Grady when he heard that. "What do we have to do? You just have to be your five year old self, and Billy there has to behave like an eight year old."

I let out a nervous laugh. "I won't be too much like I was when I was eight years old unless you want to spend some extra money on rubber sheets." Winters suddenly looked very serious, so I started talking without thinking. "I used to wet the bed until after junior high. My dad used to think that I was doing it on purpose, but I just had really bad kidneys."

Winters started to take down some notes. "Did your father punish you for these accidents?"

I shrugged. "I just wore, you know, protection. It was out of sight and out of mind...at least when I was a kid." I took a deep breath. "I moved out of my parents' house when I was still seventeen to live with Sylvia. She drank a lot, and I thought it was really grown up to drink. My dad never went to bed without finishing at least three beers first. Well, I started drinking..." I blushed, but Winters urged me to continue. "Let's just say the nighttime sprinkler system was turned on. Three months after I moved back into Dad's place, this time with Racer. Even though I was underage, I had three beers a night with my dad. I thought it made me grown up. I pretended that my sides didn't hurt afterward. Well, I started wearing protection and was too stupid to realize that I needed to cut the alcohol. Racer was being potty trained and he had an accident. I tried to be encouraging. Half way through the conversation, he pulls down my sweats to reveal that I was wearing...you know...protection. He asked my son if he wanted to be a man like him or a baby like me."

"What happened next?" Winters asked.

"Something in me snapped. I used to have a problem with my temper, but I saw a counselor. I'm doing much better."

"Did you hit your father? Your son?"

"No!" I yelled defensively. "I never hit Racer, didn't matter how angry I got. I was worried about losing it around him, so I had to let it out somehow." I felt so stupid talking about this, but it was a thousand dollars. "I started crying, sobbing on the floor in a diaper. My dad never let me live that down."

"I will keep that in mind," he said. Grady put a hand on my shoulder and Winters gave him a scolding look. "Remember that you are the younger brother."

"Yes, sir," Grady said, pulling his hand away.

"How about you, young man? Do you have any stories about being five years old? Did you wet the bed like your brother? Sleep with a particular stuffed animal? Anything of that sort that you tell me will be beneficial."

"This is kind of embarrassing," Grady said blushing. "I never slept with a stuffed animal." He bit his lower lip. "This is going to sound a lot more crazy than it actual was." He stuttered for a few moments, looking over at me nervously. "I never slept with a stuffed animal, because I slept with my dad's football helmet. I never was any good at football, but my dad used to play in high school and college. He was proud of his time in college. Whenever he saw a University of Arizona game, it was like he was the one out there on the field."

"He gave you his helmet to sleep with?" Winters asked, taking his notes very slow and taking the story in.

"My parents divorced when I was five," Grady explained. "My mom moved in with her sister. I lived with three sisters and two cousins, all girls. It was a different time. Dad was afraid that I was going to turn out...you know..."

"No," Winters said. "How was your father afraid you were going to turn out, Grady?"

"Gay," he whispered. He gave me an apologetic look. "You have to remember that it was a different time. I never met any gay people. I like gay people. My best friend is bi. I'm not a homophobe."

"So you slept with this football helmet to keep homosexuality away?" Winters said. "How old were you when you stopped sleeping with it?"

"When I lost my virginity," Grady admitted guiltily. "I was seventeen years old. If it wasn't for Regina Johnson, I would've drug that football helmet with me to boot camp."

"I think that you are perfect candidates for our experiment. You will have to surrender your cell phones. I will inform you of any emergencies. Do not worry. I have to limit outside contact to keep the experiment from being contaminated. You will have one bit of adult business and that is of shaving. Your face shall be shaved twice a day. Facial hair tends to destroy the illusions of childhood."

"So if we complete this week acting like kids we get a thousand dollars," I asked, just to make certain.

"If you are very good boys, Santa Claus will bring a very special package filled with a thousand dollars cash," Winters said.

"Just out of curiosity," I asked. "Are you going to spank us?"

Winters gave us a knowing smile, and I started to feel more like an eight year old boy. "If you're good boys, you'll never have to find out."

***

Our first taste of childhood was discovering that all of our clothes were chosen for us, even our underwear. They listened to our suggestions of stuff we liked when we were kids and stuff we liked to wear, but the choice was out of our hands.

They set us up in a fake apartment filled with kid's furniture and a couple toys here and there. We had a television, but every channel that wasn't age appropriate was blocked. The two of us had bunk beds, and I winced when they told me that I had to sleep on the bottom bunk even though I was the older brother. I recognized the telltale crinkle of plastic sheets. "That way you don't have to worry about accidents," Winters explained.

"Are you supposed to be our dad?" Grady asked,

holding the battered old football helmet on his lap. Winters made us leave everything at home, but he demanded that Grady bring his dad's helmet to sleep with.

"No," Winters said, almost sounding offended. For a brief moment, his Santa Claus façade actually looked creepy. His eyes were cold. "You boys cannot see your parents. I can't tell you why. You're too young to understand. They're not dead, but they are gone. Until they come back, you have to stay in this foster home."

"When are they coming back?" I asked, surprised at how young I sounded. My voice was weak. My mind returned to when my mom left us in the middle of the night. When I finally got hold of her, she told me that she had a new life and didn't want anything to do with me.

I looked over at Grady who was hugging the helmet tighter to his chest. A parent leaving felt like the end of the world. The less Winters told us and the way he refused to answer our questions made me feel abandoned.

"Got to get through this week," I whispered. "This must be what Racer felt when I went to jail."

"No talking!" Winters screamed. "What is your problem, Billy? Why can't you shut your mouth for just five minutes? Are you an idiot or do you have some uncontrolled mouth spasms? Maybe I should get your jaw wired shut? Do you think you could shut up then? Is that what it's going to take to shut you up?" Winters slammed his fist on the wall. "Answer the question, boy!"

"I can be quiet," I said, my voice small.

Winters eyes bored into me. I felt like dirt, less than

dirt. This man absolutely hated me. "Stay in your room, both of you." When we didn't say anything, he started screaming at the top of his lungs. "STAY IN YOUR ROOM! DO YOU TWO UNDERSTAND ME! ANSWER ME!"

"Yes, sir," Grady said first, and I echoed the sentiment.

Winters smiled, but his eyes were still cold. "Good boys. I know that you guys are going to fit in fine. Don't worry there should be plenty of food." My brow scrunched up. Grady moved off the top bunk and sat next to me. The two of us were genuinely scared. "I just have to feed my children first. You guys will get whatever's left. I'm sure that there'll be plenty."

"Thank you," I said, hoping that was the right thing.

"Such good little boys," Winters said. "Santa Claus is going to bring you a lot of candy this year. All good little boys love candy."

***

We thought Winters would be back in a few hours, but he left us alone until almost bedtime. My stomach burned and screamed, and Grady started to feel tired and fussy. We could smell the food. I hazarded the door several time, but it remained locked. Every time we thought someone was coming to the door, we perked up.

When Winters finally arrived, the food was cold and it was mainly vegetables with the remains of spaghetti the other "children" left on their plate. "There wasn't enough for both you and my children," Winters said coldly. "I had to make a choice. You're lucky that they don't like broccoli and okra." He also handed us two tall glasses of water and told us that he expected us to go straight to bed after we were done eating.

I sipped at the water, just enough to help force the room temperature noodles and soggy vegetables down. Despite his hunger, Grady barely touched his food. Whenever he swallowed, he made disgusted faces.

"Drink your water," Winters commanded me. I tried to remind him about my accidents, and he looked at me like he wished I was dead. "Drink your water or you won't get anything to drink until Christmas."

I took another swallow, trying to convince myself that I wouldn't have an accident. It was just water, not beer. "Yes, sir."

"We have a rule in this house," Winters explained. "I made it up just for you two boys. My own kids are above this rule. If one of you gets punished, both of you gets punished." The two of us nodded solemnly, and I reminded myself that it was only six more days. "That is not just punishment from me, but Santa Clause. If one of you says that they do not believe in Santa Claus, neither one of you gets the money from Santa Claus." I gasped. "Is that understood, boys."

"Yes, sir," we said reluctantly. "Only six more days until Santa Claus arrives," I reminded Grady. That seemed to cheer him up.

"You didn't eat a lot," Winters said, picking up our plates after we shoved them away. "If you had eaten everything on your plate, you would've been allowed to eat at the table with the other children. I guess you've proven that you two are just going to waste food. For the rest of the week, you will receive nothing but leftovers."

Neither of us could say anything. This seemed cruel, but I went through worse at jail. At least, no one was going to try to have their way with the pretty, blond, skinny dude.

"Did you get plenty of water, Billy?" Winters asked as he watched to make sure that I drank every drop. I nodded and handed him the glass. "Good. Into your pajamas, brush your teeth, and go straight to bed."

Long after we shut off the lights, we heard the sound of Winters playing with the other "children." I wondered when we were going to meet them, and I asked Santa Claus for one more thing before I slept. I needed this week to go as quickly as possible.

***

I was still half asleep when Winters came in before dawn and pulled the cartoon character decorated covers off me. "Did you wet your bed, William?" he asked. I blinked and saw that I had completely soaked most of my pajamas. Without protection of anything but a plastic sheet, I rolled around in my own waters during my nightmares.

"I told you about my kidneys----"

"Maybe you should ask Santa for a new kidney?" Winters asked. He shook his head and made disapproving noises. "No, you won't get anything from Santa this year. Santa doesn't give anything to nasty, lazy boys." Grady started to ask what was going on when Winters ordered us both into the front room.

"Can't I take a shower first?" I asked. The look on his face silenced me, and I dripped as I followed him into the front room.

Our room had a couple of toys and posters, but the rest of the house looked like a children's paradise: game systems, expensive stuffed animals, party balloons, candy in every dish. The other "children" were a college age student, some homeless hippie guy who looked uncomfortable shaved, and a woman in her sixties. They were dressed neat and clean. Another college student acted as their nanny while a chef provided them stuffed French toast for breakfast.

"Billy is eight years old," Winters said. "Any of you children notice something wrong about Billy."

"He's all wet," the college boy said, in a childlike falsetto. He carried a velvet teddy bear in his arms, and his footed sleeper looked cut specifically for him. "Did he fall in the swimming pool, Daddy?"

"No," he had an accident. "That's all pee on him. Billy wet his bed. Do you know what kind of people have accidents?"

"Babies," the hippie guy said.

Winters gave the boy a playful tussle of his long hair but he shook his head. "No," he cooed. "If Billy was a baby, he would be wearing a diaper." Without warning, he pulled down my pajama pants to reveal my yellowed underwear. "No diapers here. Billy is not a baby."

"I could wear protection," I said weakly.

Winters raised an eyebrow. As much as he adored his "children," he hated Grady and me. "What kind of protection, Billy? You're a bit young to be using condoms." The middle aged little girl giggled into a lace handkerchief. "Do you need an athletic supporter? I know that your little brother sleeps

86

with a football helmet. Are you two part of some midnight football league?"

"You know what kind of protection," I said defensively.

Winters shook his head. "You have to say it, Billy. If you want something, you have to properly ask." He gave a wink to his children before turning back to me. "Ask like a gentleman."

It took me several attempts to stutter it out. "I would like to wear bedwetting pants or diapers or whatever at night," I said, saying it aloud made me feel sick. "I wet the bed and don't want wake up like this." I felt gross, and I held my breath because the stench got worse with every second. "Please," I added.

Winters thought a moment. "No, you may not wear diapers, Billy. Diapers are for babies. You're not a baby. You're a worthless, lazy little brat who would rather lay in his own filth than get up and go to the bathroom. All of my children are dry."

"Then can I not have to drink so much before bed," I pleaded. "Please."

Winters stood over by the other children and they all looked down on us. "You know the rules. If one of you is punished---"

"I'll do it," Grady said. "Neither one of us will drink anything until the end of the week." He stood next to me. "A man can go a couple weeks, and I'm pretty sure that Winters isn't trying to kill us."

Winters laughed. "Don't worry. I won't let you two

dehydrate. You will both have one glass of water to share. I think that sounds fair." The two of us nodded. I needed to take a shower. As much as I hated to admit it, I wanted to cry. I hoped with the water running that Winters and the other children wouldn't be able to hear me.

"Maybe Santa Claus will bring you some pampers, Billy," Winters called after us as he sent us back into our room. The other children cackled. "I forgot to tell you that Billy and Grady still believe in Santa Claus. They think he's going to bring them a nice present. Poor and stupid kids always believe in Santa Claus, because they don't have a Daddy that loves them to buy them everything they ever want."

"There's no such thing as Santa Claus," the three children chanted in unison. We heard that long after Winters locked our door. When they tired of that, they started making up rhymes about "little wet Billy."

***

Winters and the other children left us alone for most of the week. We turned up the television, so we wouldn't hear them playing on the other side of the locked door. We pretended not to smell the food being cooked, and reminded ourselves to be thankful for the little we got to eat. At least, my bed and pajamas remained dry.

Halfway through the sixth day, we heard a key in the door. The other kids burst in wearing designer clothes. Winters bragged about how he took them shopping and they got to pick out whatever clothes they wanted.

"We've come to play with your toys," the college boy

said.

Grady shrugged and handed him a robot. The college boy quickly snapped off his head. "These toys suck. I don't want them in the house anymore." We watched as Winters came over and smashed all of our toys with a hammer in front of the cheering children.

"They are always watching television," the female said. "Everyone knows that rots your brain." She took her high heeled cowboy boots and smashed the screen, laughing like a jackal.

Grady and I remained silent and watched them destroy what little entertainment we had. "Just two more days until Santa Claus comes," I whispered.

The college boy grinned mischievously. "I want to play with that, Daddy." The hippie jumped up and down like a lunatic. I held my breath when I realized that they were both pointing at Grady's football helmet.

"No!" Grady screamed.

Winters stood in the way. "If you don't want them to play with the football helmet, all you have to say is that there is no Santa Claus. You two will leave here penniless. I hope your friend finds a place to stay."

"I'll say it," I said.

Grady shook his head. "There is a Santa Claus! There is a Santa Claus! There is a Santa Claus!" he chanted it over and over as he watched them take his father's football helmet and lock the door behind them.

"I'm sure they wouldn't really do anything to it," I said, trying to comfort him. "They know how much it means to you." On the other side of the door we heard smashing and finally the sound of something shattering.

The kids opened the door real quick and threw the pieces of the helmet inside. "Now you don't have a father any more," the hippie said. "You didn't deserve anything like that anyways."

"He's just stupid," the college boy said. I ran toward the door, but the female shut and locked it. They continued to create rhymes and songs, singing them at the top of their lungs until Winters called them to dinner.

"Are you going to be all right?" I asked. I put my arm around, and he pushed me away. He scooped up the pieces of the helmet, crying with tears or sound.

"Of course," he lied, throwing the pieces away and wiping his eyes. "It's just a helmet. It's not like I'm really afraid that I'll turn gay if I don't have it." He paced back and forth. I saw his heart sink, even as he forced himself to tell a joke. "If I do end up gay, you better become my boyfriend."

"You don't know how long I've waited for you to say that," I joked back.

I heard Grady continue to chant as we fell asleep. "I'm an adult," he said, "not a little boy." I pretended like I couldn't hear him, just like I pretended that I didn't hear him sobbing his eyes out. "I am not a little boy," he whispered until late until the night. I think he started to say it in his sleep.

When I woke up the next morning, Grady was sucking his thumb.

***

Our last day was quiet. Without a television or toys, the

90

two of us stared at the blank walls and remembered where the posters used to be. The other kids never made any noise. Winters probably took them to a mall. Neither of us felt like talking, and I jumped when Grady finally spoke. "Do you think he ran out of ways to torture us?" He moved next to me, and I put my arm around him. "I think Winters might be out of ideas. All we have to do is wait here for Santa to arrive."

I nodded, my mind cloudy. I tried to focus on the outside world. I was there just seven days ago, but it felt like someone else. "Racer," I said out loud, reminding myself of the kid that I endured all this for.

The door opened slowly, and I squeezed Grady tightly. He was shaking, and I saw his thumb try to work his way back into his mouth. "It's going to be all right," I said. "It could be Santa Claus."

Winters looked festive enough to be Santa Claus, wearing his red and green and laughing happily. "I have to say, guys, that I expected you to break. You guys did wonderfully. Thanks to you, the experiment was a success."

I looked down at my pajamas and did the best to remind myself that I was a grown man. "Don't you have to interview us or something?" I said, still using a little boy's voice. "Find out if we still believe in Santa?"

Winters shook his head and offered us our old, adult clothes. I blinked, uncertain if I should actually change. I approached the suitcase slowly, throwing the clothes on the bed and expecting them to attack me. The old man waited for us to change. It felt weird to wear boxers again. "Has it really only been a week?" Grady said, vocalizing what we both were

91

thinking.

"I know why you guys claimed to still believe in Santa Claus," Winters said, taking out two thousand dollars in cash from his overstuffed wallet. "Greed, plain and simple. A thousand dollars seems like a lot of money for someone like you. Reality shows have taught me that people will do anything as long as money is involved."

"What was this whole thing about then?" I said, feeling the anger rising inside of me. I didn't want to cry. I wanted to rip off the smirk from his face. He needed to pay for what he did to the two of us.

"I used to experiment on children, but that is so inhumane," Winters explained. "I'm still surprised at how easily I can get adults to act like children. All I have to do is appeal to the part of them that hates responsibility. I got those three to be nothing but spoiled little brats in a little less than an hour."

"I don't understand," I said, opening and closing my fists and forcing myself to remain calm. A small voice inside my head said that if I hit this bastard Santa Claus would never come and visit me.

"I wanted to prove the cruelty of children." My mouth dropped open. Grady looked disgusted. "If children think that they are superior to another child, they are capable of acts of terrible abuse. The three in there knew that there was no Santa Claus. They thought the whole notion was stupid. By telling them that you two still believed in Saint Nick, they thought that they were smarter than you. When I told them a couple facts about you, it made sense to them they were superior to you."

"That's horrible," Grady said. "Why would you do that?"

Winters ignored him. "I think it also helped that they had limited exposure to you, not that they wanted to play with you. The first night, one of them told me to stick a diuretic in your drink. They wanted to see you wet the bed."

"Then it wasn't just the---"

Winters talked over me. "They kept asking me to beat the two of you, but I think that was a bit extreme. Instead, I convinced them to just to spit in your food and feed you less. One of them asked me to put dog food in the meat. That seemed like a reasonable request. I mean, you guys were so starving that I don't think you ever even noticed."

"Did you really destroy my father's helmet?" Grady asked.

Winters shook his head and Grady eased for a moment. "No, I let them destroy the helmet. The more I told them how important it was to you, the more important it was to them that it was utterly destroyed. I could've ended the experiment right then, but I wanted it to go on the full seven days."

He shook both of our hands. "Congratulations, you have proven the utterly cruelty and prejudice within children." Winters actually expected us to be excited, and he frowned at us when we just stood there, staring.

"Is there anything you want to add?" he finally asked. "Like I said, I know why you two claimed to still believe in Santa Claus---"

"He's real," I interrupted, shoving the money into my

pocket and leading Grady out of there. "Santa Claus is real, you sick bastard. He took us from that horrible place, and showed me that I have to work hard to make sure that my kid never ends up living in the twisted world you created."

Grady looked back and smiled like a naughty child. "You've been a very bad boy," he said. "One day, you're going to be punished."

COAL
BY DALE ELSTER

Cindy Bannerman braced her hands against the small of her back and stood up straight, feeling the muscles spasm painfully under her fingers. The dense band of musculature didn't go easily, but as Cindy walked in slow, small circles in front of the wrapping table, the tension eased and she began to feel better. She was again reminded of her mother-in-law, before the cancer, before the poor woman was reduced to little more than a walking corpse, and how she repeatedly asked if Cindy was sure she didn't have a bad back.

"Only during the holidays," Cindy always replied.

And it was true.

The shopping, the cleaning, the endless baking – Cindy didn't mind any of the drudgery that came with the Christmas season. In fact, she loved it, because Christmas time meant family time, and no one loved their family more than Cynthia Bannerman. And why shouldn't she love them?

Her husband, Mark, as a successful (and highly-skilled) District Attorney, was an excellent provider. She had two beautiful children, Cole and Mary Beth, who were destined for great things in life.

And why wouldn't they be?

They were adorable, they were twins, and she was reminded every day by neighbors and school teachers alike how delightful they were to be around! They were smart, well-mannered and she was doing just an incredible job raising them!

Life for Cindy and the Bannerman clan was good.

No. Not just good.

Life was perfect!

But wrapping presents was hell.

She looked around.

There were so many!

And only one day to wrap them! Heck, only one day to do *everything* this year!

Cindy sighed, so deeply that her head dipped all the way forward, tensing the muscles in her back again. She quickly stood straight, a fit of laughter bursting up from her chest.

She was blessed! She was so blessed to have this many packages to wrap for her family! What on earth was she complaining about?

Her fit of laughter abruptly stopped.

She listened intently for a moment, halting her breathing.

There it was again.

A distant, shrill tone. Electronic. Phone? Was it Mark calling? So soon! A rush of adrenaline fueled by the sudden panic raced through Cindy's veins.

Then she remembered.

She chuckled as she identified the sound.

It was the new kitchen timer she had purchased yesterday.

She raced down the stairs, ignoring the images that flashed through her mind – not of burned cookies and the precious loss of time – but of her old kitchen timer hurtling through the air, and the gash opening across Mark's forehead. The splotches of blood on the clean white tile.

Those negative images were wiped away by the warm vanilla aroma of her famous sugar cookie recipe as she hurried across the kitchen and pulled the trays out of the oven.

Cindy smiled, inhaling deeply.

Perfect!

She transferred the cookies onto a wire cooling rack with all the others and then hurried back upstairs to finish the wrapping.

She checked her watch.

Less than an hour now!

Fifty-six minutes to wrap the gifts, arrange them under the tree, decorate the cookies and make the eggnog! And there were still the children to get ready!

Cindy stood still in front of the presents that littered her bed and drew in a long, soothing breath of cinnamon-scented air from the candles burning on the night table in the corner of the room. She let it out, rolling her shoulders around to unknot the tension building up in them. The action deducted a whole minute off her allotted time, but she didn't mind. A tiny therapeutic moment for herself was just what she needed.

It had been one helluva day so far.

"We've been in worse time crunches, Cindy," she said

aloud to herself. "C'mon now, we can do this."

She got to work.

Twenty-two minutes later, the remaining presents were wrapped and carefully arranged under the tree, a stunning nine foot Douglas fir adorned with both inherited and purchased ornaments carefully selected to complement each other. The lights were tastefully white and non-blinking, casting the room in a comforting glow.

Cindy didn't take much time to be proud of her hard work. Even though she had made great time with the presents there was still a long way to go.

She placed her hands on her hips, considering her next move.

Cookies or kids?

The Famous Cookies.

Earlier in the day she had arranged her kitchen island with all the ingredients and tools she would need to knock out the cookie decorating. Small bowls of homemade frosting of various colors were lined up in neat rows along with spreaders, sprinkles, decorative sugars and antique silver platters waiting to receive the finished product. It was all very efficient.

Martha Stewart had nothing on Cindy Bannerman!

Cindy had a tendency to whistle when she was rushed for time. As her small, manicured fingers deftly worked the spreaders and piping bags, she whistled "Jingle Bells" in that same soft intensity that permeated her personality.

Cynthia Bannerman was nobody's fool.

Piercing blue eyes. High cheek bones. Lips that

exhibited a natural fullness without being too large. She was a beautiful woman, and being beautiful endowed her with a certain power that all women of physical beauty possess, but few master, as she had.

At Mark's work, the men wanted her body and their wives wanted to be her, and Cindy manipulated each of them without ever coming off like a slut or a cold-hearted bitch. Each of them was like the tools in her kitchen – they all had a use, and they all had their place.

She placed the last cookie on the tray and, still whistling, delivered it to the dining room, placing it on the freshly polished cherry dining table.

Eggnog.

It was done already, minus the booze. The time crunch had forced her to doctor up store bought eggnog this year, an act she would have found intolerable under any circumstances in previous years, but her husband had left her no choice. He had broken their routine. He had altered the plan.

Cindy pushed that thought from her mind.

That situation would be dealt with later.

She had allowed the children their sampling, minus the booze of course. It had done the trick. Each year they looked forward to her eggnog and cookies, and even though it wasn't the official start of the Christmas Eve festivities yet, this year Cindy had let them have a small plate of cookies and her famous eggnog in order to quell their excitement.

Each year the Bannerman family was allowed to open one present each on Christmas Eve; part of a family-only celebration that included cookies, eggnog, canapés, and other

99

equally fabulous hors d'oeuvres Cindy had spent the day making. She had insisted that Mark have the tedious office holiday parties out of the way well before Christmas Eve arrived.

No business associates or politicians allowed, thank you very much!

Of course he did as he was told.

She always got what she wanted.

Until this year.

Cindy went to the kitchen and hefted a large glass pitcher out of the Sub-Zero refrigerator. As she exited the kitchen she grabbed a bottle of rum from the island. She carefully poured the milky contents into the punch bowl on the dining room table, added a quick splash of rum, then after a moment's consideration, added a generous dose before fishing a whole nutmeg and micro plane out of the pocket of her apron. She held the tool over the punch bowl and grated the spice onto the surface of the eggnog.

There. Perfect!

She dropped the micro plane back into her apron pocket and cleared away the pitcher to the smaller of the two kitchen sinks as the phone rang.

Mark!

She snatched up the phone from next to the refrigerator, her thought confirmed as she saw her husband's name and cell phone number displayed on the caller ID screen.

"Sorry, Cindy – the office party is running a little late. I'll be there shortly."

"How shortly?"

There was a sigh on the other end. Then a pause.

Checking his watch, Cindy surmised. *Or Janelle Sherman's ass. Bitch.*

Sensing the sudden tension, her husband attempted to diffuse it by changing the subject. But it wouldn't work. The stress of her recent marital status — not to mention her very busy day — was knotted inside her, clenched like a fist inside her chest.

"So – are the kids excited?"

"Excited about their mother being ripped away from them you mean?"

"We've been through this, Cindy. C'mon, now. Let's just focus on what was agreed – having a nice family Christmas."

Too late. Cindy could feel herself losing control. All the stress, all the frustration, all the sadness – *oh that goddamned sadness* – a stew of emotions that she had locked away for so long was now building up inside her like a pressure cooker. It was going to explode.

She couldn't let it.   Not yet.

Hold on, she screamed silently inside her mind. *Hold it together, Cindy! Just a little longer now!*

She dropped her right hand to her side and breathed deeply in and out for a few seconds, the phone clutched against her chest. The house smelled of warm cinnamon and sweet vanilla sugar. The aroma soothed her, settled her, like a violently boiling kettle simmers down when gently stirred.

She smiled as she raised the phone to her cheek.

"I'm sorry, Mark – you're right," she chuckled. "Of course you're right. We'll have one last Christmas together. As a family."

"We'll always be a family, Cindy. I hope you know that. It's just – the circumstances will be different, that's all."

"I know."

Mark's voice suddenly brightened. "I got Cole that snow board he's had his eye on – you know, that Shaun White model? I know you were against the idea—for safety reasons—but I just couldn't help myself! I picked one up! I want to give it to him tonight!"

"Oh? Well, he'll be thrilled," Cindy flatly replied. She was gripping the phone so tightly her knuckles her bright white.

"Tell you what," he continued, not noticing the sudden shift in her mood. "I'm ditching the rest of these stiffs as soon as I hang up, okay? I think I'm well over the legal limit for small talk," he added, chuckling at his own joke. "See you in ten minutes, Cin!"

"Perfect," she replied.

Ten minutes.

Christmas Eve. Small town traffic. Or lack thereof.

He'll be here in six minutes if he leaves right away. Which he won't. He'll be more like fifteen minutes by the time he spreads around the usual nicey-nice-hugs-and-holiday-wishes bullshit.

Perfect.

Cindy eyed the bottle of rum. Snatched it up and unscrewed the cap and downed what would have been the poured equivalent of three fingers worth in one, nearly seamless motion. Then she wiped her mouth with the sleeve of her special Christmas sweater as she climbed the front staircase.

Kids.

Twenty-eight minutes later there was a wash of headlights across the dining room.

Cindy had finished with hauling the remaining gifts down the stairs, as well as all the last minute fussing with the details, a full two minutes prior to Mark's arrival.

She was now in the sitting room (the room for adults only) awash in soft candlelight. The room smelled of peppermint. Cindy basked in the atmosphere.

If Mark remembered the tradition – and she was confident that he would – he would come to this room first while the children played quietly in their rumpus room on the other side of the house.

He didn't disappoint.

"Hello, Cindy."

It was a scene repeated each year, the script written from that first family Christmas nearly a decade earlier.

They sat together on a loveseat sharing quiet conversation and the best eggnog either of them had ever tasted.

Except this year.

Mark made a face after a long sip of his.

"Strong."

"You don't like it?"

"No, it's not that," he quickly replied. "Not that at all."

"But?"

"It's just stronger than you usually make it, that's all."

"If only I'd had more time . . ."

He sipped more. "No no—it's good stuff," he lied.

Cindy didn't mind.

She wasn't drinking hers.

"This is nice," she said, indicating the atmosphere of the room with an upward tilt of her head.

"You've outdone yourself once again."

A quiet moment passed as they enjoyed the room.

"Want to know something?" she asked him.

"Sure."

"I really wish you hadn't taken the kids from me."

"Now Cindy—"

"I really wish you hadn't gone to the authorities, Marcus. I wish you hadn't labeled me as a crazy person incapable of caring for her own children. I really wish you hadn't done that."

Cindy was nonchalant in her delivery. There was no tension in her voice, no inner rage roiling under the surface. Maybe it was the booze.

"Remember what we talked about, Cindy. We're ending this like adults. Spending Christmas together. Let's just keep our focus on that, okay? Let's not ruin it."

"Too late."

Mark sighed heavily in exasperation and then stood up. "Fine," he said. "I'll drive you back to your apartment. Katy can stay with the kids."

"No!" Cindy rushed to her feet and grasped her

husband's arm with both hands, a desperate, pleading expression distorting her otherwise flawless features. "No, please! You're right! I'll be civil, I swear! Sit back down, now – finish your eggnog."

Mark complied, reluctantly.

"Speaking of Katy – is she still here? I hired her until 7 o' clock."

"I sent her on her way. I don't need a nanny's help. I can take care of things myself."

Mark finished his eggnog and placed the empty glass back on the end table, checking that it was centered on the provided coaster.

"That's just the point, Cindy. You've been so – "

"High-strung?" she interrupted. "Isn't that the term you like to use for me now? High-strung or tightly-wound or something polite like that? Something that sits well with the boys at the country club, hmm? I bet you used far more official terminology when you arranged for temporary sole custody with Judge Lattimore, that fat shit buddy of yours. Didn't you Marcus?"

Mark's handsome, genial features squeezed tightly in anger as she spoke. Just as she finished speaking he shot forward in his seat, closing up the small distance between them.

"Christ, Cindy – what did you expect me to do?"

He wanted to shout, but, conscious of the children being nearby, kept his voice low.

"I covered for you as long as I could!" he continued. "After what you did to those cats—not to mention the dog!

105

What did you expect me to do, Cindy? It was bad enough I had to lie to the children about what really happened to their pets! Then you refused to get help—"

Mark took a pause to keep the argument from escalating further, wiping the sweat from his forehead with a hanky pulled from the inner pocket of his blazer.

"Let me say this," he began again, his voice more calm. "If you hadn't hurt Mary Beth, we wouldn't be having this conversation. Everything would have been fine."

Cindy burst into tears.

Mark hesitated, then placed his hand on her shoulder and offered his handkerchief, hoping to quickly calm his wife without raising the children's suspicions.

"At least you're getting help now, Cindy. I give you all the credit in the world for that. You've shown a great deal of progress these last several weeks."

"Yes," she sobbed, wiping her tears. "I have been feeling better."

Within a minute's time, she had stopped crying and, other than a slight redness in her eyes, looked like the same old Cindy Bannerman again.

"You gave me Christmas," she said as she quickly embraced her husband. "Even though the doctor advised against it. That was sweet, Mark."

"No one wants things to be like they were more than I do, Cindy. Believe me. But they can't. You and I both know they can't. It's just – just such a crazy time of year to be alone, you know? I couldn't do that to you. You're the mother of my children, for God's sake."

There was a sound coming from the other room.

Laughter.

The kids!

Mark's face brightened.

"I think they're onto your plan this year," he laughed.

Cindy stood. Took her husband's hand.

"Come," she said. "Let's go see them."

As they made their way down the hallway toward the living room, Mark's grip on her hand tightened.

A convulsion. In his abdomen.

He stooped over, bracing himself against the wall. A thick, milky cord of drool spilled over his bottom lip, splashing onto the hardwood floor.

"What the hell did you do to me?"

"Secret ingredient," Cindy whispered. Although her husband wasn't looking at her, there was a prideful expression on her face. "Really compliments the rum, don't you think?"

"Bitch." Mark had trouble forming the word. It groaned out in a tangle of sound, his throat closing up by the second. But she understood him. It wasn't the first time he'd used that word lately.

"Oh Mark," Cindy chummily replied, swinging one of his arms over her shoulder. "Let's get you sat down."

He was growing dramatically weaker with each step, but ever since the separation, Cindy had upped her workouts to five days a week. She easily bore his weight.

"Those office Christmas parties will be the death of you," she told him as she guided him toward his favorite chair, a beautiful antique wing-back with matching ottoman, positioned squarely in front of his sixty-inch flat screen.

The TV. His children. A video of Christmas morning the previous year.

His real children were sitting on the couch.

No. Not sitting.

Arranged.

Bloody foam still bubbling up from their open mouths.

The same foam that was now beginning to escape his own lips.

Mark tried to scream, but he was too weak, fighting hard for breath.

"God! Oh, God no!"

He struggled to get out of the chair, to rush over to them, but that urgency was expressed in barely more than a stiffening of his arms before the muscles slacked and gave out altogether, plunging his weight down into the cushion of the chair again.

"Kids," he said, trying to shout the words, to scream, but all his body could manage was a harsh whisper accompanied by a liquidy wheezing noise.

Cindy stood over him, glaring down at his face.

"You did this!" she screamed.

All the rage she had been holding back burst out of her with a vengeance.

"You! You killed them, not me! It was you who killed this family, Marcus! You!"

She was holding a Christmas stocking in her hand. Her husband's name was neatly embroidered in the white cuff.

She turned it upside down. Small black objects spilled out onto his lap.

Coal.

Her rage suddenly spent, Cindy's voice took on an odd, scolding tone, like a prissy 19th century schoolteacher disciplining a young child

"This is all you get for Christmas, Marcus Bannerman!"

Her husband's eyes flared, his breath hitched in his throat.

Cindy stood over her him a moment longer, and when his lungs failed to snatch up any more of the pine-scented air in the room, she let out a contented sigh before stepping away from him to sit down on the couch between her children.

Her babies.

She watched the video with her children snuggled next to her on the sofa, delighting in the surprised looks on their faces as they came tromping down the stairs in their pajamas and discovered all the presents Santa had left for them. Cindy included her children in her near constant running commentary of the action displayed on the screen as if they were living participants in the discussion. Instead, they simply sat alongside their mother in silent agreement.

Then she took her attention off the video and looked down.

There were matching square boxes on each of their laps, wrapped in shimmery red paper with handmade bows of shiny green satin.

"Presents!"

Mary Beth's chin was tilted upward toward the ceiling.

"Here. Let mommy help you, darling," Cindy said, wedging one of the seasonal throw pillows behind her daughter's head. The young girl's open but vacant blue eyes were now fixed on her mother.

Cindy manipulated her daughter's hands to mimic the girl's presentation of the proudly wrapped gift to her mother.

She lifted off the lid, drawing in a tiny breath of feigned surprise as she peeked inside.

"For me? How sweet you are, Mary Beth! Yes, Merry Christmas to you as well, my darling little girl!"

Inside the box was a single bullet.

Cindy held it in her hand, admiring the way the lighting from the tree caught the bullet, glinted off the metal casing.

Like a tiny ornament, she thought.

She turned to her son.

"Why Cole," she smiled in mock bashfulness. "You shouldn't have!"

Cindy took the box from his lap and opened it. Inside it was a gun. A .38 snub nose revolver. Stolen from her husband's "secret" hiding spot.

"It's just what I wanted!"

Cindy Bannerman always got what she wanted.

"Merry Christmas to all," she shouted gleefully as she loaded the single bullet into the gun.

She wrapped her arms tightly around her children, hugging them close so that the barrel of the gun could make firm contact with her forehead.

"And to all a good night!"

110

THE CHRISTMAS WISH
BY CRYSTAL CONNOR

He thumbed through the list on the screen of his phone one more time just to be sure. It was confirmed. An emergency addition. He looked again at the naughty list and sighed. It seemed to get longer and longer with each passing year. And this year, there were more girls than boys. Tonight all of the gifts for the good children had been dispensed before the hour of the night had reached double digits, the fastest time on record.

The problem with Christianity was forgiveness, but rest assured, there would be none of that here tonight. The moon was already halfway between the zenith and the western horizon and he still had almost a million children to deal with before the sun rose.

The wide-eyed little girl he had tied up and put in front of the fireplace had black ringlets that hung just past her shoulders. Her big brown eyes were just a shade or two darker than her skin. She looked like an angel. He ignored her tears, walked into the kitchen, and helped himself to another cookie.

The little girl was scared, but there was nothing she could do to free herself from her nylon imprisonment, so she just glared at the intruder while he ate the cookies that she and her little brother had left out for him.

111

She knew this man was Santa, because she had seen the sleigh against the backdrop of the moon, heard him coming down the chimney, and watched him step out of the fireplace. She knew he was Santa, even though he was like no other Santa she had seen in pictures, at the mall, or on TV.

He wasn't fat, and the last thing he looked was jolly.

He wore a metal helmet, his long red hair had gray in it, and so did his beard, but he wasn't old enough to have all white hair. He wore a black nightgown with a wide red belt tied across his flat belly, but she could see what he had on underneath because it didn't cover his sleeves and it wasn't very long. The gown was worn over black pants, a black sleeveless shirt, and black boots. The man eating cookies in the kitchen looked more like Thor than Santa.

The big red symbol on his chest was the same symbol that was on his shield: one line going up and down with five slanted lines drawn across it. The word above the symbol said 'AUTHORITY,' and the words under the symbol said 'and OBEDIENCE.' The words formed a circle around the strange symbol. The only thing that was the same as with the others she'd seen were his eyes ... They were blue.

Santa ate the last cookie. Overlooking the glass of warm milk sitting next to the cookie-crumbed saucer, he went to the refrigerator and drank straight from the cartoon. With his thirst satisfied he returned to the living room and took a seat in front of the bound girl. Even when seated, Santa loomed over her. The girl's eyes flickered. Her breath was labored. He knew the small child was going to pass out. At six years old, she was the youngest child on the list, and without a doubt

112

the most frightened child he had seen, not only tonight but in a long, long while.

He grabbed the little girl by the collar of her pajamas that displayed a little black princess holding a frog and removed the ball gag that was entirely too large. She took a long, deep, relieved breath.

Unlike the other children on this list, she did not shrink from him.

"You're not *really* Santa. Santa's nice; he would never do this." A large tear slowly fell from her eye. "You look like him, but you're not really him. Are you Santa's son?"

He leaned forward, and with a calloused thumb, roughly smudged the tear from her face.

"My name is Kris Kringle and these," he said as he licked his thumb, "are not going to help you. I do not have a son. I am here because you're on the naughty list ... for the second year in a row."

"Well, I got a dolly last year!" she stated with an indignant huff.

"Last year you were too young to be disciplined." The child's eyes drifted from the angry orbs of ice down to the third word blazed upon the front of his tunic: 'OBEDIENCE.'

She took a deep breath and tilted her head in thought. She held the gaze of his ice-blue eyes once more. She tried stretching her shoulders, but with her hands firmly tied behind her back she couldn't move them very far.

"It's Christmastime; you're supposed to be nice."

"Really, Says who?"

"Says *Jesus!*" Clearly the young girl was outraged by

Santa's ignorance.

"Hmmm." Santa leaned back and crossed his legs. "After *all* that you've done, *now* you want Jesus?"

She thought about it for a moment and decided that she didn't. Santa read her internal dialogue like an open book. She was trying to think her way out of this. Santa was no longer surprised that the child before him was an emergency addition to the naughty list.

"So then, am I getting a spanking?"

Santa laughed. He was sure that if she had locomotion, she would have asked that sassy question with a hand on her hip.

The rod had been spared in this household, and they were well beyond the niceties of corporal punishment. The behavior of this child demanded a return to the old way of things. Tonight, this babe would be reborn upon the altar of dutifulness.

Father Christmas and his young hostage looked up in response to hoof stomps. The animals on the roof were growing restless, and the old saint was behind schedule.

Most people neglected to remember the dark origins of the holiday and therefore failed to realize the consequences of being on the naughty list, which was reviewed and edited several times a year. Santa did more than just bring gifts and eat cookies. Children, like their parents, forgot or did not know that, above all else, Santa was a disciplinarian and that clumps of coal were useless tools when it came to child behavioral modification and teen attitude adjusting.

He reached for his bulky bag.

Santa laid the contents in a neat row at the feet of the ill-behaved princess and gave his watch a quick glance. Looking at the items placed before her, the child began to cry.

The pear of anguish was not sugar coated, and the mere illumination from the night-light made the metal gleam. Men using enhanced interrogation techniques would have protested the horrors. What was a little girl to do?

"Santa," she said with terror-filled awe, "I have to go potty." As Mr. Kringle slowly stood to tower over the child, a trickle of warm liquid ran down her legs to form a puddle that pooled around her small feet.

He turned his back to her tears and began to pace while being careful to not walk through the blood. Even with this carnage, this savagery, he pulled out his phone and checked the list once more. Just to be sure. Using his thumb and pointer finger, he enlarged the image on his screen. The picture he was looking at was a mirror image of the little girl crying behind him.

Santa returned to the kitchen, took a plastic cup from the cupboard, and filled it with sweet liquid. He grabbed the towel from the handle of the refrigerator and knelt before the young girl he had come to punish.

He allowed the young one to soothe her dry throat with the cool juice from the forbidden fruit that had caused the fall of man. He removed the rope that held her wrists behind her back and clamped a strong grip to the back of her neck. He marched her into her bedroom, found a fresh pair of pajamas, and then led her to the door of the bathroom.

"Go clean yourself up."

115

When he heard the running water, he returned to living room to stand over the dead. Chills ran down his spine has he tried to come to terms with how a six-year-old child could kill a man the same size as he or how one so young could kill her own mother.

He didn't hear her, but he knew she was there because he could smell her. He turned to face the strawberry-scented child. The depth of the detachment with which she regarded the deceased was alarming. The only emotion she displayed was reverence when she looked up to Santa's face.

"Do I still have to get a spanking?" she asked again on the brink of tears. Rustling behind the couch commanded Santa's attention, and he tossed the furniture aside to reveal a boy child, smaller and younger than the girl. The boy fled from his hiding place, stood behind his sister, and gawked up at Santa through a mask of bruises. The bridge of his nose was red, under his eye was purple, and the color of his cheek was blue. Santa watched the movement of the girl's eyes as they drifted over the decaying with contempt.

"Do you know about Santa's helpers?" he asked as he glared down at the children. The boy was nodding yes while his sister spoke for both of them.

"They're the elves who live with you in the North Pole and work at the toy shop."

Santa swore. In days of old, children were afraid of elves and rightly so, for they were vicious deities responsible for nightmares, diseases, and death. It was the elves that kept track of those who had been nice and those who hadn't.

It sickened Santa to think that when people thought of

elves, the image that came to mind was that of colorful, diminutive, playful things of children's cartoons. It was no wonder that people where astonished to learn that being on the naughty list was a way of illustrating that actions had consequences, that those consequences required penitence, and that the debt had to be paid in blood.

The true assistants of Saint Nicholas were demons dispatched to avenge injustice or insult, descending from long and amazing family trees, which included Gods of the North who flew through the sky with the help of horses, reindeers, and goats.

With Belsnickel, he had a judge. With Zwarte Piet, who was personally in charge of the naughty and nice lists, he had a jury. With Lapland, the Wildman who bashed in children's skulls and drank from their necks as soon as he delivered gifts to the undeserving, he once had an executioner. Le Père Fouettard, who killed children, cut them up and put them in a stewpot, replaced Lapland, but like the Wildman, Le Père Fouettard was no more.

Santa was gently lured from his thoughts as he noticed how the child protecting her brother lustfully eyed the cat-o-nine. The sparkle in her eye matched the glint of the razor-sharp barbs. Her eyes lovingly caressed the manacles before they fell so assiduously upon the bastinado cane, a tool used to inflict a particularly brutal and cruel form of punishment in which the soles of the feet are whipped. She slowly took a visual inventory of all the instruments that would be used for the implementation of acceptable behavior, and smiled.

Santa had been mourning the loss of Fouettard for

thousands of years, but Santa would yearn no more. This girl child who stood before him would replace Le Père Fouettard just as Le Père Fouettard replaced Lapland, the Wildman.

Santa's Christmas wish had been granted. Once again, after all these years, Santa had an executioner.

It was time to return to the old way of things.

GETTING TOGETHER FOR CHRISTMAS
BY ALLAN IZEN

People were everywhere, thronging the crosswalks overhead, crowding the galleries, swarming through the central court, esplanades, concourses and plazas, milling about in neon-lit shops and coffee bars and boutiques.

None of them were me.

But I *had* to be here somewhere!

I'd stopped by the mall after work to finish up the Christmas shopping. I hate malls so I hurried to get it over with. In and out of the toy stores, I hooked gifts into my basket for nieces and nephews. I made a pass through the bath shop, dashed into Borders for a copy of *Goodnight Moon*; hit the clothing outlet stores for t-shirts and a pair of daisy-patched jeans.

Joanne wanted me home by seven to watch the kids while she went to rehearse with her recorder consort and for once it looked like I was going to make it.

Laden with bundles and bags, I staggered out of the mall and started across the parking lot searching for the hindquarters of my car. A wet blustery wind was slapping me in the face; it was dark and mist swirled in the air. I could hardly see a thing.

There was an explosion of pain as I was hit hard from

119

behind. The lights went out, the projector went off and I fell out of the world.

Slowly I came back, wracked in pain.

I pried my eyelids apart and found myself face-down in a puddle, unable to lift my head. With all the strength I could muster I managed to roll my head to one side. That got my mouth out of the filthy puddle water and I was able to sip a tiny breath of air.

Behind me a car was idling, the glare of its headlights flooded the asphalt around me, lighting pebbles and scraps in glaring white light. My lizard-brain panicked at the sound of a car engine on top of me and in a torrent of adrenalin I dredged up the strength to crawl away from the car.

I got to my feet and stumbled away until I collided with a parked Jeep and fell onto its flat rear bumper. Crushed by pain, I began passing out again when something caught my eye: There was a second body on the asphalt, surrounded by scattered packages. My packages.

Where had *he* come from?

Had this goddamn driver hit two of us? The miserable son of a bitch had to be drunk or wrecked on drugs.

The guy on the ground looked bad, like a sack of ripped-open laundry.

The car door opened and an elderly man in a windbreaker climbed out. He leaned in the car and told someone to stay put, he'd take care of it.

He bent over the man on the ground, gingerly put fingers on his neck and assumed a listening posture. After a moment, he rolled the victim on his back and put an ear to the man's chest.

It struck me as odd that the driver paid no attention to me. Certainly, the guy on the ground was worse off than I was, but that bastard of a driver had clobbered both of us, you'd think he might deign to spare a nod in my direction.

There was something odd about this. Maybe it was the victim's clothes, a Snowfield jacket with lemon shoulder trim. His khaki slacks were torn and filthy and his Rockports had been knocked off his feet. They lay on the asphalt behind him.

The fact was…he was dressed like me.

And he was kind of stocky.

Also like me.

I got off the bumper and did a spaghetti-legged shuffle over to him. My pain seemed to be letting up a bit. I took a look at the victim and my heart began to pound.

It *was* me.

On the asphalt like a shattered doll, one arm flung to the side, the other bent backwards at the elbow.

There hadn't been two pedestrians.

And the driver wasn't ignoring me out of rudeness; he didn't know I was there.

He called over his shoulder, "Annie? Annie, call nine-one-one."

He stood up and swatted the grit off his trousers.

I watched with a chill in my heart. If I were dead shouldn't I be flying down a tunnel into a blinding white light?

Then the man on the ground – me – groaned and rolled onto his stomach. Painfully, scrabbling with his shattered arms, he pushed himself weakly onto all fours. His hair was plastered to his forehead; his face was a hash of raw skin and mud. He looked around, dazed and blinking.

The driver hopped back, alarmed.

The man on the ground struggled to his feet and hobbled off slowly, teetering from side-to-side as if doing tai chi.

"Hey," the driver called, "I called nine-one-one. You better stay here, buddy. Hey!"

But the injured man heaved himself forward, lurching zombie-like into the parked cars.

I hadn't the slightest idea what was going on, but somehow I knew I couldn't let him get away. I seemed to be having some kind of out-of-body experience and I knew that if I lost my body I would lose my life.

So I started after him, moving with elaborate caution to minimize the agonizing pain. But to my astonishment, once I started moving the pain evaporated, as if by magic. Soon I was jogging lightly, following my body as he (should I call it an *it*? No, it was my body) bounced clumsily into cars, banged into bumpers and hung himself up on side mirrors.

He was making for the mall, so I ran ahead to wait for him outside the entrance. When he came out of the parking lot, I moved into position, planning to nab him before he could lose himself in the mall. What I would do then I had no idea, but I wasn't going to let him go.

He reeled tipsily out of the parking lot, gyrating toward me. I got ready, started toward him but at the last minute he juked to one side and fled into the mall.

I charged after him and immediately became bogged down in an ocean of Christmas shoppers. Harried mothers were chivvying their wailing youngsters. Teenagers in hoodies and headbands rambled loosely through the crowds, jiving and cursing. There were elderly mall-walkers, security guards and characters of all kinds thronging through the esplanades.

In the commotion I couldn't see my body.

I worked my way through the crowd into a hall the size of an airplane hangar. There was neon everywhere, food kiosks offering Thai food, tacos, won ton, sushi, burgers, pizza, pretzels, yogurt, juices, cinnamon buns and Korean beef. Pop music blared; the air was heavy with food smells. Steel picnic tables were welded to the floor. People sat shoulder-to-shoulder, hunched over their Styrofoam boxes, plastic cups and glasses.

But nowhere did I see him.

I moved out into the central courtyard, a huge space filled with dwarf trees in planters, ferns, stone benches, foam Santas, garlands of ribbons and colored lights, cherubs tooting trumpets, banners and golden bells everywhere. In the center, a tiled fountain plashed under a rotunda four levels above.

I plowed through the crowds but saw no sign of him. The view would be better from the second level so I headed for the escalator muttering 'scuse me' over and over as I pushed through the masses.

It quickly became clear though that there was no need to be so polite. No one was actually blocking my way. Not that anyone intentionally stepped aside to let me pass; they all just sort of flowed past me as if I weren't there.

I rode the escalator to the second level, stood at the railing and looked down on the central court. The mall was built on a triangular motif, three broad concourses radiating out from the center court like spokes of a wheel. Each of them went up four levels, blazing with light and clamoring with Christmas cheer.

A feeling of futility spread through me as I took it all in. Talk about your needle in a haystack; how could I ever find a single person in this sea of humanity?

Obviously I needed a strategy. I figured that my body, wherever it was, would be causing a stir. What with his lurching gait, flopping arms, torn clothing, blood and filth, he was sure to be attracting attention. I decided I'd do better to stop looking for him and look instead for the disturbance he'd be making in the crowd.

"Yer workin' too hard, man."

It was almost like someone had spoken to me but since I'd returned to the mall nobody had even noticed me, much less spoken to me. I looked behind me and saw a huge man breasting the crowds, making his way toward me.

He was a bearded, big-bellied, ham-handed, scowling bear of a man with a drooping moustache and a greasy do-rag. A biker, he stood six-foot-four, at least. Tattoos swirled up his brawny arms like pastel smoke. And the shoppers melted out of his way as they had done for me.

He walked up to me with a baleful look.

"Gah damn," he said in a gravelly voice, "I seen you down in the court, man, pussyfootin' through the citizens like you din't have no sense at all. When I seen you tryin' to get on the escalator I said to myself, shit, man, this dude is a raw recruit if I ever seen one. How long you been here anyway?"

What on Earth was he talking about?

"How long have I been here in the mall? I don't know, five minutes? I just came in."

"No wonder."

"No wonder what?"

I was frantic to get back to my search. My body was getting farther away by the second. On the other hand, I didn't want to annoy this man.

"Look," I craned to one side, trying to see into the central court below, "I don't want to be rude but I'm trying to, uh, find someone."

"'*Find* someone?" he scoffed. "Who you tryina find? And what are you gonna do when you find 'im? Hate to tell ya, dude, but yer dead, y'know."

"Dead?"

"As a mackerel. So relax. There ain't nobody you gotta see, no place you gotta be. Not anymore."

Dead?

It made a certain depressing sense, and maybe on some level I'd known all along, but damn it, I didn't *feel* dead. Except for being scared shitless, I felt fine.

I'd sort it out later. Right now I had bigger fish to fry.

"Listen, uh . . . "

"Mouse."

"Mouse?"

"My name."

125

"Ah, okay Mouse, look –"

"An' you are who?"

"Charley. Charley Lewis. Sorry, Mouse, but I have to get going."

Mouse shook his head. "I don't think so, buddy, you're dead. Get used to it."

"Okay, look, it's true a car knocked me down in the parking lot. But I got right up. How could I do that if I were dead?"

Mouse shook his head slowly as I told him the story. The more I talked, the more I realized how lame it all sounded.

"So I got off the bumper," I blathered, "and all of a sudden the guy on the ground, me, I suppose you'd say, he jumps up and runs back to the mall with me chasing after him. So how exactly am I dead?"

"Splittin'," Mouse nodded sagely. "I seen it happen before."

"Splitting?"

"Yeah. It happens when you get hit hard but not hard enough to kill ya. Your body thinks it's all over so it lets loose o' yer spirit, astral body, yer soul, whatever you want to call it. But sometimes yer body *doesn't* die and there you are, trapped outside with no way to get back in."

Mouse softened.

"Hey, it ain't such a bad life, bein' dead. You kin hang with me, buddy. I'll show you the ropes."

I took a longer look at Mouse. Beneath the matted hair and menacing stare, Mouse had a simple, fubsy face, almost

126

kindly.

"Kind of a shock, ain't it?" he said. "Everyone goes through it, though. I was just talkin' with Alfredo this morning. He's a maintenance worker who got killed a few months ago. And his pal Carlos. He fell off a ladder puttin' up the Christmas lights just a couple of days ago. An' there's a bunch of old people, too. They come to the mall to walk, get their exercise and all and their hearts just give out. There's one now, Rose. See 'er?"

I looked in the direction he was pointing and saw a grandmotherly woman in a bombazine coat and babushka peering at the Radio Shack display.

"Yo, Rose," Mouse called.

She turned and gave him a cheery wave. "Hello, Mousie."

Mouse turned to me and said, "Yeah, people die all the time here. Me, I got cracked outside the tire shop a couple months ago. They put a tire on my bike. I *told* the little bastard in the office I'd pay at the end of the week, but he wouldn't listen. I got pissed, jumped on my bike and took off. So the fuckin doofus pulls up the security spikes and I wipe out. Landed wrong.

"Bummed me out, man. I just walked around the mall for days, watchin' everybody coming and going, buyin' shit, eating. Stuff I'd never do again. I felt like I got kicked out of the circus." He sighed. "Hey, there's ol' Florence."

He pointed to an elderly woman down in the central court. She had a cottony tuft of hair and wore baggy slacks, a Nylon pullover and sneakers. There was a translucence about her.

"She's fading," Mouse said. "When you been here long enough you start to fade. Ol' Florence won't be around much longer."

Despite my fascination with the things Mouse was telling me, I was still on fire to locate my wayward body.

"Mouse," I pleaded, "I really gotta go. I got to find my body."

"Your *empty*, you mean. We call 'em empties. Bodies without no one inside 'em. You can try, I guess, but you better be quick. They don't last long. Empties are totally stupid, y'know. They get hit by cars, they fall out of windows, walk through glass doors, drown or get electrocuted or whatever. And when yer empty dies, that's it for you, too. You got no place to go. You're dead once and for all."

"Once and for all? You mean I'm not dead *now*?"

"Technically no," Mouse replied. "Yer sorta *half* dead."

"If I'm not all the way dead, then I can get back, right?"

Mouse shrugged. "Splitters always try, but none of 'em ever made it that I ever heard of. Except one guy. I heard he pulled it off, but that's probably bullshit. A legend or something."

"How did he do it?"

Mouse scratched his beard. "Well, what I heard was, he was up here on the second level when he spotted his empty down below. He got real heavy, jumped off the deck and landed on his empty so hard he sorta busted back in.

"But that would be hard to do. Empties are hard to catch, man. If they see you comin', they'll run."

I recalled how my body had juked around me in the parking lot. It looked like my chances of reuniting with him were small and shrinking by the second. I stared bleakly at the throngs below and – wonder of wonders – *there he was.*

The shoeless raggedy man in the filthy jacket and torn pants, shoving people aside as he wandered aimlessly through the crowds. Actually he wasn't shoving too many people out of the way, he didn't have to. They couldn't get out of his way fast enough. Mothers grabbed their children and hauled them out of his way as quickly as they could. Everyone was avoiding him. His woozy path took him across the center court and he was about to start down one of the concourses.

I had to act fast.

Spotting him among all the people down there was an incredible stroke of luck, but if I didn't get down there in time I might lose him. This was my big – probably my *only* - chance to go on living.

"Mouse," I said, "you see that idiot waltzing around down there? That's me – that's my body – I gotta go."

I scooted around Mouse and started toward the escalator.

"Not so fast, champ."

Mouse materialized in front of me. I ran smack into him and bounced back. He may have been a ghost, nut he was rock-solid to me.

"Hey," I protested.

"Like I said, Charlie, I'm takin' care of you. You got to learn about bein' dead, man, you can't just luck up on it. Catchin' yer empty may be hard, but to have any chance at all you got to know how."

"Mouse, what are you talking about?"

"Like for instance, you don't have take the damn escalator down to the court. You can just *go* down there, man. If you keep on doing things the old-fashioned way, walkin' around and ridin' the escalators and shit, you'll never catch 'im."

"Mouse," I was wild to get away, "I gotta get going. How am I supposed to get down there if I don't take the escalator?"

"What you do is you sorta *think* your way down there. Picture in your mind where you want to go. Then scrunch up and wish real hard and it'll just happen. Try it."

Crazy? For sure, but crazy was my life now, so, to humor Mouse, I squeezed my eyes shut and imagined myself rising into the air and flying over the center court. After a few seconds I opened my eyes to see how I was doing.

No change; I was still standing in front of Mouse.

"It didn't work," I cried. "Now will you let me by? He's getting away."

"Naw, man, you want to catch him just go down and hover over him while he runs around. He won't get away."

"Look I just *tried* that, okay? And it didn't work. I can't do it."

"Sure you can."

Mouse grabbed me by the belt and collar, hoisted me over his head and heaved me over the railing.

Dead or not, I'm terrified of heights.

"Hey!" I screamed hysterically, sailing out over the

crowd. "Are you crazy?"

"Just kickin' you out of the nest so's you can fly, little birdie."

I was turning in the air like a scrap of tissue. My feet were over my head. I looked down to see the rotunda below, center court revolving over my head. I would have been screaming in blind panic if I'd had anything to scream with. But after a minute or so, I opened my eyes and saw I wasn't falling.

I was floating.

"Way to go champ!" Mouse yelled from the gallery.

Thrilled and terrified, I did a timid dogpaddle in the air and had a second revelation: I didn't have to swim; I didn't have to move my arms and legs at all. As Mouse had said, all I had to do was *think* myself along.

So I experimented, thinking myself up a bit higher, down a little lower, forward, back, side-to-side. The freedom was exhilarating, but I couldn't lose sight of the task at hand.

My body had gone stumbling into one of the concourses, so I swooped after him, gliding over the crowds with my arms in front like Superman. I scanned the host below, tacking from side to side, checking the shops, rising occasionally to make a sweep of the galleries above.

I couldn't find him.

I sailed along to the end of the concourse where huge glass doors opened onto the parking lot. I somehow had a feeling he would stay in the mall, so I turned and started back, searching frantically as I went.

Finally I spotted him.

A turbulence in the river of shoppers was parting, as if flowing around a rock. I went down for a closer look and sure enough there he was, doing an ungainly adagio to music only he could hear.

"That you down there?"

Mouse was suddenly coasting in the air alongside me.

"Yeah," I said. "That's me."

"Jeez, man. You sure you wanna get back into *that* puss-bag?"

Mouse had a point. My body looked to be in terrible shape. If I got back in I might be dooming myself to a life of disability. But still...it was my body, it was me. I had to try. "Yeah, I do," I said. "I wish I could figure out how."

"Well," Mouse offered, "the guy I told you about, he dropped on his empty, hit him so hard he just kinda crashed in. That's the only thing I ever heard that worked."

"Dropped on him? How did he do that? I mean, we're just spirits aren't we? Do we weigh anything?"

"Well, he made himself heavy. It's hard to do."

"How did he do it?"

"You make yourself solid. You can only do that for a minute or so. It takes a lot energy and you have to stay focused. There's this guy, you'll run into him sooner or later around the mall. His name is Homer. He was a Buddhist monk, a smart dude. He explained it to me once. He said when we die we turn back into some kind of energy that we always were, 'animated air' he called it. But we can get back to something like a living body if we want to. You got to make yourself solid and that's real hard to do, like I said. And once you get a little heft, it's hard to hold onto it."

As I listened to Mouse, I never took my eye off of my body as it goofed around the central court.

"So what you're saying is . . . what *are* you saying?"

"I'm sayin' you gotta hit him hard, Charley. You gotta git up there an' drop like a bomb."

The idea of dropping on anyone, much less my own body, made me queasy.

"I don't think I can do that."

Mouse shrugged. "What are you afraid of? Dyin'?"

The man had made another good point.

I eased down to the floor and squeezed my eyes shut, visualized myself growing heavy and pretty soon I began to feel . . . strange.

Things around me began to change. The colors grew brighter, the background noise, the hum of the mall, became louder. But most surprising of all, I was cold. I hadn't noticed it, but since returning to the mall I hadn't been feeling anything temperature-wise. I hadn't been cold, hadn't been warm either.

In fact as I grew more solid, the world of the senses enrobed me once again and it was wonderful. Voices grew sharp, the clamor and Christmas carols grew clear and loud, like a symphony. Children were chattering and laughing and bawling, conversations were humming all over the place, announcements were booming out of the mall speakers. There was a guy sitting on the wall of the fountain playing a guitar. I'd never heard anything so beautiful.

And then, to my complete amazement a woman

bumped into me. She gave me a quick smile and murmured sorry.

She had seen me, felt me. As if I were alive.

But Mouse had been right about needing lots of energy to do this. I was exhausted. As wonderful as it was to taste life again, I had to conserve my energy for the main event.

I let it go and immediately reverted to my former state of 'animated air'.

I rested for a few minutes, then decided it was time.

I rose over the center court and tried to hover over my body. It wasn't easy. He was lurching and staggering erratically. I tried to get above him and move slowly in front, leading him.

When the alignment was as good as I could get it, I shut my eyes and started putting on the pounds. I felt myself falling, picking up speed as I piled on the weight.

I looked below and to my dismay saw I was going to miss him by a mile. I aborted my efforts and once again became a puff of animated air.

I'd be damned if I'd let him get away though.

I put myself on the floor behind him, as he did mad pirouettes. I grew solid and started through the crowd, moving up fast behind him. Suddenly he turned and saw me. Our eyes locked for an amazing second, then he lurched away.

Although I was weighed down by my heaviness, his aimless capering made it easy to get closer to him. I was closing fast, ready to clobber him. Exhaustion overwhelmed me but I pushed it back. There would be a huge energy debt to be paid later, but I wasn't worrying about it at the moment.

I got ready to summon the last of my strength and lunge and started toward him in a ponderous fast walk. Then he did it again, he spun tipsily to one side and I clumped harmlessly past him.

He seemed aware of the danger I posed and set off stumbling toward the fountain. I followed behind, my feet stamping ominously on the tiles like monster feet.

"Heads up, Charley."

Mouse suddenly materialized in front of my body, moved in fast and clobbered him with a ferocious body block. That stopped my body cold. He stood there, teetering, ready to fall.

I was running as hard as I could; I launched myself into the air as if I were making a football tackle. Just as my feet were leaving the ground, Mouse moved in and shoved my body at me with a force that doubled the impact of our collision; I hit him like a barrel of wet cement and…

…something hard went soft, letting me in with an almost sexual penetration. Then there was a sharp, tearing pain and an icy chill and I was suffocating, desperate for air.

I gasped and I inhaled a chestful of water. I thrashed wildly, and I knew I was in my death throes. I was going to die this time and all this agony had all been for nothing.

I opened my eyes and saw I was on my back in shallow water. I pushed up to a sitting position and found myself splay-legged in the fountain breathing like a ripsaw. Blood and mud were leaking into the water around me.

I hiccoughed, belched out a ropy arc of water. I

followed this with a medley of gagging, vomiting, and drooling.

Not a lovely performance to put on for the public, but who cared – I was alive.

Shoppers massed around the fountain looking at me with a variety of expressions. I could imagine how I looked to them; a filthy, bleeding, bum sitting in a public fountain surrounded by vomit doilies.

Alive. Alive. Alive.

A security guard rushed to the edge of the fountain.

"Get out of the fountain, sir," he ordered.

I tried to comply but couldn't manage it.

"Are you okay, Sir?"

I nodded, retching and coughing.

He put a foot on the fountain edge and held out a hand. I took it and he pulled me to a standing position and steadied me as I sloshed out of the fountain.

A second security guard came with a wheelchair and blankets. The two of them eased me into the wheelchair, draped blankets around my shoulders and legs. One of the guards, Gary, according to his name badge, asked if I could talk.

I tried, but only made noises like a train making an emergency stop.

The mall doctor arrived with a policeman, Sergeant Merrick. While he examined me, Sgt. Merrick opened his notebook and started asking questions.

I cleared my throat and coughed, but I couldn't produce a single word.

"He can't talk," the doctor said. "He swallowed a lot of water. It's heavily chlorinated."

A narrow-shouldered woman in a cloth coat, her iron-gray hair in a tidy bun, bustled up to Sergeant Merrick and told him she'd seen the whole thing.

"He came in at Sears," she said. "Someone said he was hit by a car but I think he's just drunk. I mean look at him. Tsk. He went prancing all over the mall like a crazy man, scaring the daylights out of everyone. He got into in some kind of a scuffle at the fountain here, I didn't see it really, but he fell in and now there's all that . . . all that *you-know-what* floating around in there. Disgusting."

Gary the security guard began wheeling me through the crowd. He said he was taking me to the doctor's office for some tests.

Sergeant Merrick was taking the woman's statement as we passed. I heard her telling him that I ought to be locked up because I was out of my head.

But I wasn't. Not any more.

And besides, it had been the other way around.

As they rolled me away I looked up to see Mouse in the crowd. His moustaches angled up as he smiled and gave me a thumbs-up.

I raised my arm to wave back, but he was gone.

THE LAST NOEL
BY ALEX AZAR

Why have you never wondered where Santa's elves came from? They're introduced to us as children and we grow up already comfortable with the notion that this jolly fat man has a race of pygmy slaves in his isolated snow kingdom. Well I'm here to answer all the questions you didn't think to ask; like why an ever-young hottie like Mrs. Claus stays with that portly home invader?

I went through all the typical stages of Christmas myths every other American does, other than the Jews, of course. Sure I believed in Santa religiously as a kid, waiting wide-eyed in bed for my gift list to be fulfilled. That faith slowly gave way to doubt over the years, only to be shattered in an awkward moment of revelation. We've all had that moment, even though the details differ. Some of us saw our dads sneaking back away from the tree in a cheap facsimile of the iconic red suit, or had a classmate ruin it for us by opening their big mouth, marking the beginning of what will be months of ridicule for still believing the obvious lie.

Or is it a lie?

After filling my son's head with the same absurdity he was taken from me at the age of four, before he could even discover the truth, by some disease that I still can't pronounce correctly. But the pain of his death was too much for my marriage and my wife left me for a world tour of foreign cocks. Feeling like I was utterly destroyed, I got sloppy and was fired, or "let go", from my job as a blog journalist.

At this point you might be asking what my sob story has to do with Santa. Well on one particular Christmas Eve the shit that life threw at me drove me to the edge and I decided to jump off. Literally. Miraculously, I was saved before hitting the bottom. Disorientated, it took me a bit to realize where I was.

Santa's sleigh.

"You have no idea how hard it is to time a catch like that. Let's not try it again, okay?"

The real-life, non-mythical Santa Claus saved my life mid-air and quipped about it. Aside from his cavalier attitude, his voice is exactly like you imagined as a child. "You've been a good boy Sammy..." Oh my god, I can't believe he actually says that, "...you don't deserve what's happened to you, but unfortunately I can't give you what's on your list. Darryl is dead; I can't bring him back."

He sees the obvious disappointment in my face and places a giant mitted hand on my shoulders. Despite its size, his hand feels almost weightless. I think he smiles but it's hard to tell through his beard. You can barely see his mouth open when he talks. "I am sorry about your son, and while I can't make it up to you, how about a different gift? Here."

He gives me the reigns in his hands and for the first time I notice reindeer floating in air before the sleigh, "Holy shit... sorry to curse sir, but this is a lot to take in. How is this even possible?"

"It's just reality, different from and yet very much like your own. Now give the line a good whip and tell these fellas where you want to go. Anywhere in the world."

Excited, I start to ask, "Even…to…"

The big man cuts me off in as polite a manner as possible, "Yes, they can take us to the moon and beyond, but you wouldn't survive the trip."

"Ah makes sense. Ok…uh…on Prancer?"

"No, no. Those aren't really they're names. Just say the destination and they'll do the rest."

A little more disappointed than I should have been, I dropped my shoulders. "Ok." It takes me a moment to think of where I want to go, but of all the bucket-list locations that came to mind like Paris, Japan, or Italy, they all feel too romantic to go with Santa and that's when it hits me. What better place to go with Santa by his reindeer? "Take me to the North Pole."

Santa laughs with a "Ho Ho Ho," that makes the hair on my neck stand giddy, "That's where they all pick."

I go from giddy to jealous faster than I would have thought possible, "What do you mean 'they'?"

Once again placing a weightless hand on my shoulder he explains, "I chose you Sammy for a reason. I'm sure you know that this time of year the rate of suicides sky-rocket and while I'd love to, I can't save everyone. But I saved you because I have a favor to ask."

"Of me?"

"Your situation and your former profession make you

the perfect person to ask. Every few generations one person is chosen to reintroduce the legend of Santa Claus to the world. My image has become a shill for corporate sponsorship, but you're going to use your journalistic abilities to invigorate the 'myth'." He finishes his sentence with air quotes, which I typically hate, but seeing Santa do it is warming, possibly because of the mitts he's wearing.

I'm about to ask him what exactly I'm supposed to do when I notice how cold it's gotten. Seeing me try to warm my arms, Santa suggests, "Look in the bag of gifts behind you, I have something with your name on it."

Reaching into his velour bag, which is deeper than it looks, I find a heavy winter coat. Sure enough, the tag hanging from the zipper has my name on it. I put on the coat and the chill just melts away. "Wow, this is the warmest jacket ever. Thank you sir."

"Please call me Santa, or Chris, or Papa. Different people I've picked up over the years choose a name more relatable to their countrymen."

"Hmm, well if it were up to me…"

"It is up to you, as of now, my entire lore is up to you. No pressure, Ho Ho Ho." He jokes, but it is a lot of pressure.

"Ok then, as an American, I'm partial to the classic, good ole Santa Claus… it's…" the rest of my thought trails off as does the air in my lungs and surrounding space.

Santa takes the reign and cracks the whip with what looks like anger in his eyes. "Hey you shits, I told you when I've got someone in here with me you can't fly so damn high!"

The sled drops altitude and air returns to me. "Thank

you, Santa." The display of anger throws me off. While it's a natural reaction for anyone, I imagined Santa Claus to be above freaking out over such thing.

"These shitheads almost killed Josefina a few weeks back. They think because they're immortal I won't punish them."

Choosing to focus on the only thing in those statements that wasn't negative, I ask, "Is Josefina Mrs. Claus?"

"Ho Ho Ho, no she's this fine piece of Brazilian tail that's got that Memento thing going on. Poor chick can't remember she bangs Santa every few months so she can't tell anyone about me. Ho Ho Ho." The bass of his laugh vibrates in my lungs, but I don't find the joy in it I did just minutes ago. "I like you Sammy. Feels like I can be myself in front of you."

He answers my next question before I can ask it. "I don't think we should include this in your new myth, huh?" I simply nod in agreement, but the journalist in me questions the integrity of the facts.

I don't have much time to dwell on my dilemma as we've arrived at the North Pole. "It's not cold anymore, but we're surrounded by snow. How?"

"Ho Ho Ho, you don't expect me to live in perpetual cold, do you?" His logic is sound but the reality of a warm Santa's workshop baffles me more than flying reindeer. "You don't have to understand something for it to be true."

The profoundness of his words washes away the weight of these events, at least temporarily, which gives me an idea. "That's your selling point. 'Just because we don't understand it, doesn't mean Santa's not real'. We use that and we could tell any of the details we want about you, no matter how fantastical."

We land in a hanger/barn and Santa reasserts what he said earlier, "Sounds good. Remember this is all up to you," Waiting for us next to the parked sleigh is a Christmas-themed golf cart.

After driving us out of the hangar Santa asks, "What do you want to see? We've got the workshop, or the naughty/nice computer. Usually people ask for the bathroom first."

Weighing my options carefully, and while I do have to take a piss, I opt for something else entirely, "Can I interview Mrs. Claus?"

"What have you heard?" He quickly asks with a sneer. Upon seeing my shock, I assume he's re-evaluating what my intentions may have been. "Of course you can, but it might be better to wait for that."

He said it as if he was spewing venom and it makes me feel that she's going to be worse than he is. Changing my course of action, I inform Santa, "Well, since I was planning to commit suicide, I haven't eaten all day. I'd love a bite to eat." As soon as the words dance off my tongue it dawns on me that I doubt I'd be able to even keep food down. This exposed Santa is more than I can take.

Without hearing a response from him, Santa maneuvers the cart into a large hotel-esque kitchen. "In here I have a full catering staff of elves ready to cook whatever you'd like 24/7; they don't sleep."

"Elves are real? Okay wait, I'm willing to accept that you have some magical barrier hiding your North Pole home in a tropical paradise, and that you have a breed of reindeer that can fly with the aid of fairy dust or some other bullshit you're keeping from me. But how is it possible that there's an entire race of jolly midgets willing to do your business all day year round?" I must not have breathed during all that because once I stopped I became light-headed.

"Ho Ho Ho oh my Ho Ho Ho. I never said anything about them being jolly and it takes a lot of... let's say persuasion...to make them *willing*." He does the stupid air-quotes thing again before waving one of them over.

Waddling like a penguin, over comes a midget whose head barely comes to my waist, but his stiff hat is the height of my nipples. "Yes master, how can I serve you?"

Answering for me, Santa orders two plates of chicken parm over spaghetti. "I love that shit, hope you don't mind." Shaking my head, he leads me over to a large dinner table and nearly ten minutes later we're served two delicious looking plates.

"So, you hinted there's more than persuading them to work with you. What's behind that?" I ask with the best of intentions but get lost in how amazing the food is.

With sauce in his beard and a noodle hanging from his mouth, Santa waves over another elf. This one is similar in height but his features are softer beneath the same foot-long beard. "This is Albina. She's been with me for nearly eight hundred years." That explains the more feminine eyes, but now my head is filled with images of seemingly-gay dwarf sex.

She lifts her beard to reveal a pendant on a thick chain and Santa continues, "Each one of the elves has this gem that bequeaths complete control to me via a larger gem in my chambers."

"So you've enslaved an entire species? That's horrible. I can't believe it."

"That's why all the other chroniclers I get sugar coat the existence of the freaks." He pats Albina on what I guess counts for an elven ass, and it's clear from the sadness in her eyes that his hand had more weight to it then when he patted my shoulder earlier. "These little bastards weren't doing anything before the Miss and I found them deep beneath the surface." He says with a mirth in his voice that you'd expect from Santa, but the subject matter is enough to turn me away from the rest of the food before me.

Unfortunately, he decides I need more details, "They lived in these frozen caves naked as the day they were born. With no sense of value they spent their days making these beautiful sculptures from precious stones they mined. We offered them a chance to share their work with the whole world, but they have some fanatical devotion to the gems. That's when the Miss discovered their 'god', a giant rock that can control them."

"So you enslaved them to make gifts for the entire world? That doesn't make sense. Why do it?" From what I've seen Santa isn't the most altruistic person out there. This just seems completely out of character, but I'm scared to ask why in fear that he'll stop altogether.

For a man of his size it's surprising to see him push away his plate before finishing every scrap of food. He says in an uncharacteristically serious tone, "At this point you're probably put off on how big of a douchebag I am but I wasn't always this way." Resettling his weight, the fat seems to bear down on him more than before, "I used to be the jolly image you dreamed of as a child, but it's impossible to be eternally happy. Now I do just enough to perpetuate the myth.

"Remember everything I once meant to you when you were a child. And then you just drop me because none of your friends still believed. Imagine how that feels, then multiple it by four billion!" The final words sounded like they carried the same weight his feet did.

Just as I start to feel sympathy for him, he shatters the delusion by letting out a belch worthy of his girth and hollers Albina's name reminiscent of a drunken husband wearing a wife-beater. This tainted image of St. Nick makes it easier to call him on his shit, "Well, I'm done eating, and you haven't given me much to work with. Perhaps Mrs. Claus can shed some positive light." I stress the word, 'positive' hoping my feelings affect him in some way, although I seriously doubt they would.

He gives me the stink eye before agreeing. "Ok, but no funny business."

As if everything else wasn't enough, his cryptic references concerning his wife only serve to confuse me further and all I utter is a weak, "Ok".

I'm being led by an elf down a long hall and suddenly realize that Santa's not with us. The elf notices my confusion and he says over his shoulder, "He and the Miss don't spend any face time together. Their relationship isn't what you've been led to believe."

With that, I finally understand all the backwards glances every time I mentioned his wife. Before I can ask for further details, the elf stops short and points at a door to our left, one door among dozens in the corridor. I take this as a sign that this is my stop, but suddenly grow weary. "All of this just seems off. Do you think I'm doing the right thing?"

For the first time, the elf turns around and I see one eye is covered with a patch and the rest of his face is heavily scarred. "You wanna do the right thing? Either kill tubby and the Miss, or kill all of us elves." Once again showing me his back, this unnamed little ball of anger walks away.

Out of foreseeable options I hesitantly enter Mrs. Claus' room. Or so I thought. Crossing the threshold I emerge into what can only be described as a sex dungeon.

The room is mostly dark, with strategically placed lights illuminating various torture devices in which elves are strapped into. The elves have tattered shreds of clothing, if any at all, and many are severely bruised and bleeding. In the center of the room is the woman I've come to question. Dressed in skin-tight, red leather and wielding a horse crop, she's a beautiful woman appearing to be no more than thirty years old. It's at this moment my mind registers the difference between Mrs. and Miss.

She locks eyes with me like a cheetah spotting a gazelle, and she's at my side just as quick, "Mmm, I haven't had a full-size toy in ages." Not until she's right up next to me can I truly appreciate how tall she is.

Before looking up to meet her gaze, I tilt my head down to see she's wearing four inch heels, but she's still towering over me by at least a foot. I swallow a lump in my throat, hopefully nonchalantly, but I see her eyes bounce with my Adam's apple, "Uh…"

She angrily slams her hands on her own hips causing the crop to brush against me. I shudder to think where that's been. "You're not here for me are you? You must be another damned reporter. Has it been that long already?" Waiting for a response that doesn't come forth, "Well, what lies are you going to tell about me now?"

As confidently as I can, I straighten my shoulders and reply, "Santa brought me here to make him and you look good. What would you like?"

"Me? All I want is someone bigger than my pinky." Running her crop between my thighs, into my crotch, and hitting the peak, she asks, "Is that you?"

Stepping away from her, I defiantly answer, "No!" Seeing her raised eyebrow, I correct my words, "I mean yes, but I just want to get all this over with so I can go home. You're all freaks!" Covering my mouth in fear I've overstepped my position.

Conversely, she throws her head back laughing hysterically. "Freaks are those who don't embrace their true nature. Like you for instance, most people would have run out at first sight of what's in this room. So let's skip all pretenses and explore your nature after the fat man falls asleep."

I'm not sure what my answer was, but suddenly I'm

back in the hallway being escorted by a different elf. He's leading me through halls I don't recall walking before. We round a corner and walk into a swarm of elves.

They surround me with a shared look of anger mixed with desperation. Emerging from the crowd is the scarred one with the eye patch. "Have you considered my offer?" Reading the confusion on my face, he elaborates. "Them or us? Who are you going to kill?"

"What? No, I'm not a killer; I'm a blogger for Pete's sake." I try to back away but their numbers condense behind me. Fear setting in, I find myself repeating things. "I just want to finish this so I can go home. I'm not a killer."

A cocked eyebrow rises over his eye-patch. "Didn't you try to kill yourself earlier today?" He turns around and walks through the crowd as they part a path for him. It's evident I'm meant to follow.

I truly believe I can jump over the first row of elves blocking me, but they're lined up six deep and look more than strong enough to hurt me. Resigned to my fate, I mutter the now familiar, "Ok" with sunken shoulders.

Walking into a dark room with a war-hardened elf is easily the scariest thing I've done. And that includes jumping to my death. "Listen, I'm sorry, but I don't know what you expect of me."

Folding his arms, the elf's muscles ripple from years of toil. "Name's Jub. And I don't expect you to kill all of us, so that leaves…" He begins moving forward, as if pushed from behind. A glow appears from under his beard, "Damn it, that bitch is calling me. Tonight, go to her room, and at midnight break the controlling rock. We'll do the rest." Jub continues out of the room echoing his sentiment, "Break the rock!"

Not even sure I want to see the Miss again; I ignore his request and ask, "Where are you going?"

Mimicking me, Jub doesn't answer.

Suddenly, many of the other elves follow suit and I'm left with a manageable amount. Sifting my way through those that remain, I'm moved by their pleading eyes. "Hey guys, I would like to help really but I'm not even sure what to do."

A single elf emerges from the group, old in the face, but relatively young with no facial hair. She looks up at me with soft eyes and pleads, "Break the rock."

At that point the decision was taken out of my hands. I resolve to help this little girl, who in reality was older than my great-grandfather would be. Patting the top of her hat, "I'll do what I can." I turn to walk away but a thought occurs, "Why don't you all just take off the gems? Wouldn't that break their control?"

An older, slightly taller male elf joins the girl before me. With a hand on her shoulder he explains, "The Miss can tell whenever one of us removes the gem. They kill whoever does, and they don't do it quickly." The girl turns her head into his chest as he continues, "Her mother was killed 300 years ago in front of all of us as an example for the rest."

The group around me collectively lets out a sigh of pain and two of the elves take my hands, one of whom I recognize as Albina. The other one says, "The fat man wants us to bring you to him to finish the tour before retiring for the night."

Leading me out, Albina squeezes my hand drawing my

attention to her. "You have to find a way to get to her room; it's the only way to save us."

I'm brought to a door with a green painted wooden sign that reads "Workshop". I don't see any sensors, but as I near it, the door opens like in a sci-fi show. The doorway opens into a football field sized factory floor.

From where I'm standing I can see elves working on bicycles, dolls, even touch screen tablets. On the opposite end sits Santa atop a lavish throne of red, green, and gold, and adorned with antlers I assume used to belong to a reindeer.

"Sammy, my man, you get all you need from the she-bitch?" Santa asks as his pimp cup is refilled by an elf standing on the shoulders of another.

Approaching him, "Actually she was busy... uh entertaining guests. She asked that I return in an hour or so."

"Yeah, she goes through them quicker than I do using them for target practice." Nonchalantly, he produces a rifle that was concealed next to his seat and takes aim on an elf building a video game system. With no hesitation, he pulls the trigger sending a bullet through the oblivious target's head.

Immediately the elf's vacant stool is occupied by another who is crying as he wipes blood of his new task. The others around him visibly shake trying to ignore the loss of one of their own.

"Want a shot? Very cathartic," Santa passively asks. Seeing the concern on my face he rationalizes, "They're hundreds of these shits. No one will miss him."

Forcing my focus away from the death, I respond, "Um no thanks. Think I'll just walk around the floor, gather what I can here." I spend the better part of an hour working from station to station, letting as many as I can know that I'm going to help them.

After forty-five minutes Santa calls me back over. "Have a drink with me." He hands me a cup with a liquid that smells stronger than turpentine. "Let me give you some advice. I'm sure the Miss'll try to seduce you, and you're probably already tempted, but if you sleep with her she will kill you. However, if you reject her, she'll only hurt you. Trust me."

I find it hard to trust anything he says, but there's some backwards logic that actually convinces me this makes sense. "You got it, Papa Noel, no sex with the Miss." I take a sip of the drink and it sends me into dry heaves and coughs of flameless fire.

Recovered with the aid of several glasses of water, I'm now standing before a door I know in my heart I'd rather not enter. But I've made my decision and I use the memory of those desperate faces I made promises to, to steel my resolve.

Reaching to knock on the door, it slides open much the same as the workshop. On the other side of the door is the Miss standing in all her glory, wearing barely-there negligee and holding a sprig of mistletoe above her head. Not waiting for my reaction she pulls me close and kisses me deep as the door closes, sealing my fate. As the kiss lingers and her hands roam my body, my determination melts away like the wax of candles around us.

Still with no words exchanged, she leads me to her bed forcing me down with a strong push. Lying on my back I see

152

what must be the rock controlling the elves. It's glowing the same dull orange and is sitting atop an intricately carved wooden stand. The sight reminds me of my mission, but I quickly forget again when Miss Claus reveals what her lave clothing was concealing.

My only saving grace at this point is that my clothes are still on, but suddenly two female elves come into sight and being undressing me. Shocked and disturbed, I jump off the bed and press myself against the dresser across from the bed. "What the hell are they doing here?"

"I thought you'd like an extra set of hands... and other body parts. Don't let their size fool you."

"That's disgusting. Ew, just...no!"

"If you prefer..." Miss claps twice and from behind a curtain emerge two male elves, "...other tastes."

My stomach twists and folds sending me backwards where there is no room. Bumping the dresser, I watch as the wooden stand slowly rocks, eventually tipping over sending the rock crashing to the floor. It lands with a louder thud than expected, but remains intact.

I move to finish the job but Miss Claus intercepts me, holding the gem close like a baby. Her eyes frantic, drill holes in me trying to determine if this was intentional.

Together our eyes shift to the rock as the quiet sound of a crack spreads, and the glow fades away.

She turns her attention away from me in time to see the four elves in the room pounce on her. I stay long enough to hear the Miss' screams get drowned out with the sound of her choking on her own blood.

I run through the halls, trying to retrace my steps to the workshop, and arrive in time to see a swarm of elves closing in on Santa. He's too distracted to notice me, so I just watch as the real-life, non-mythical Santa Claus is torn apart, piece by piece. While most of the elves are content in killing their oppressor, there are a few that eat the parts they've severed.

The spectacle continues for well over an hour, but it's clear the fat bastard died within minutes of the attack. Once there was nothing left to grab hold of, the elves, en masse, turn their attention to me.

Surrounded by a horde of elves, they all begin taking off the controlling gems and stare at me intensely. Not sure if their pleased I help them break free, or if I should fear their wrath for giving into the Miss and only freeing them accidentally, I prepare to wet my pants.

Again Jub appears from the crowd and stands before me, looking up to make proper eye contact. And that's when I realize...I killed Santa on Christmas day.

A CHRISTMAS DIRGE
BY JASON M. BLOOM

Matthew was dead; of this much his brother was certain. One day he seemed fit as a fiddle, the next, moldering atop a pile of bodies stacked like cord wood in the frigid air. It was a wonder why such a delicate wooden instrument would be the model of health, but there it was.

No sooner had he been bitten by a man who seemed to rise from nowhere in the gloomy, fog-covered street, Matthew began exhibiting strange symptoms: twitches and tics, heart palpitations and a slight foaming at the mouth, tingling in his extremities and heat which radiated from his body in waves. The profuse sweat ran in rivulets from him, pooling beneath his well-worn shoes and darkening the cobblestones below.

Edward knew he was dead, being his next of kin, his closest ally, his only ally. Matthew had little in the way of friendship to bestow upon others, and Edward had none at all. The two were brothers all right, but now, Edward was truly orphaned and sole proprietor to their shop.

After his death, Edward continued to run the shop by himself, keeping his head down, driven with a single-minded purpose. Not because he was trying to bury himself, lose himself in his work, not to forget his grief, goodness no, but simply to make money. He had not even bothered to take his brother's name off the wooden sign which hung above the shop door: Edward & Matthew Oremor; Proprietors. There it hung for years afterwards, and although Edward would occasionally be called Matthew, he never corrected them. Why should he? After all, wasn't it business he was here for? It was certainly not idle conversation.

Tomorrow would be Edward's fifth Christmas alone, ever since that day when Matthew was bitten and subsequently infected on that fateful night by the strange man, by the zombie. No one knew how the creature had gotten into the town, the night patrol was flummoxed, the inspectors baffled, and the townspeople a little shook up. But it wasn't the first time a ghoul shambled its way into their fortified little hamlet, and it might not be the last. But, to be sure, they doubled the guard and began checking darkened alleys more closely, and it seemed as if the gaslights burned just a bit brighter.

The town even adopted an early warning system, coincidentally invented by Matthew before his untimely demise. He invented many things in the town, which made Edward appear smaller by comparison. He never invented anything; he only kept the books and counted the money. Matthew was the driving force behind the town's elaborate entrance gates, power plant, even the sanitation system. He had also suggested the night watch survey as large an area as possible, so small hot air balloons were tethered to the enormous wall that surrounded the town, each containing a watchman who signaled down to the guards if they spied anything suspicious. Both the balloon's envelope and basket were coated in dark paint so they would not be easily spotted against the night sky. They would, as one would expect, cast a large shadow which blocked out the twinkling stars, but to the eyes of the shambling dead, this was but a small thing.

But Edward hardly ever looked up; he was constantly looking down at his feet to ensure no time was wasted shuffling between home and work, down at his hands to ensure each coin counted and accurately recorded in the ledger, and down at his fireplace to ensure each small lump of coal was not foolishly tossed in. He detested waste and no matter how cold it got, even if his hands shook to draw in heat, he refused to succumb to creature comforts, to grow soft and yield to wasteful desires.

Even now he raised a tattered sleeve and wiped his pointed nose, a small dribble of mucus already crusting there. He wore a loose dress shirt, threadbare in places with a frayed hemline underneath an ill-fitting suit jacket made of thin cloth with stains across the back, showing lack of care at where he sat. He was not a clean man, becoming even messier in the years after his brother's passing, and having never married, no one advised him or suggested alternatives in the way of clothing.

As it were, this frugal man worked as long as he could until the lights dimmed too low to see. Finally he allowed himself to trudge homeward, locking the shop, the sign swinging slowly above his uncovered head. The sky grew dark with storm clouds, knitting together like a troubled brow. Edward took care to avoid the darkest corners of the alleyways and picked his way slowly to his house, a squat two-story affair crafted of rough-hewn boards covered with large sheets of metal. They were slopped with too many coats of dark paint, like nearly every building in the town, giving the place a drab look. There was also a heavily reinforced door and thick iron bars which covering the small windows, his own personal touch. Just because he was frugal did not mean he had a death wish; he was no easy prey, either to his patrons, his creditors, or the undead bodies roaming freely in the pale moonlight.

As Edward approached the door a violent chill ran through him, the hairs on the back of his neck rising up. He pulled at his jacket, clenching the fabric in his bony hand, and as he glanced upwards he could have sworn he saw the outline of a face in the grain of the wooden door, just for an instant, and then it was gone. He blinked, clearing the image of his dead brother's face from his mind, unlocked the door, and stepped into the darkness.

***

Edward reached for another small lump of coal and tossed it into the tidy fire before him. He stoked it with an iron poker and sat back with a grunt, falling into the overstuffed chair with ripped-up arms, the stuffing peeking through the tears. He pulled at his robe and shook his sleeve back as he took up the can of soup he was eating from. He had warmed it near the flames and was eating directly from the dented can, which came from a stockpile near his bed. He spooned another mouthful, the flickering light from the fireplace reflecting in his dark eyes.

He felt a draft of cold air blast through the room and

furrowed his brow, being the sort of person who would get annoyed at the weather, something entirely out of his control. Truly, that was the crux of it; if he could not force his will upon it then it should be removed from his sight, shunned, or considered beneath his notice. The weather, the townsfolk, the corpses that stalked the lands beyond the wall, all of it were out of his control, and thus, not a part of his mind. But things were about to take a dramatic shift, beginning with the creak upon the steps beyond the door to the small upstairs bedroom.

There it was again. Another creak, then a rough dragging sound, shuffling up one step, another, followed by a thump. The handle jiggled the key still in place just below the tarnished brass knob. It twisted left, right, and then stopped. Edward's eyes were fixated on the door, and was about to breathe a sigh of relief when the loud pounding began. Insistent, the sound drove itself deeply into Edward's head, his blood pulsating with each bang. He was reaching for the fireplace poker when the door began to buckle, swelling outward as if inflating like the skin of a balloon, stretching so much that Edward instinctively put an arm up to shield himself as the door shattered, fragmenting into a million splinters and showering the room like falling snow, as Matthew stepped through the twisted door frame and limped into the room.

***

Edward's eyes widened but his mouth barely moved, just the corners twitched upwards in a smirk, as if he somehow expected to see his dead brother once again.

159

Matthew shuffled into the room, dragging his right leg behind him and holding his arms out for balance as he hobbled towards the chair opposite his brother. Edward sat back as the zombie approached, his hands outstretched, but Matthew simply gripped the chair and lowered himself onto the threadbare cushion. A dirty rag was tied around his head, knotted at the top of his skull, holding his mouth shut. His skin was a pale parody of its previous ruddiness, waxen and pallid, not unlike rotten meat. The former rosy glow was gone; indeed, even his brother's eyes were dull, devoid of luster and emotion. Some measure of stubble coated his face, and his fingernails were long and cracked all telltale postmortem signs. With his sunken eyes coated in a blue-white haze and his lips gray, Edward knew with certainty that this was indeed his brother back from the grave. Yet, here he was, sitting calmly across from him, not elbow-deep in his intestines. So why was he here, if not to feast upon his warm flesh?

Almost as if he could hear his thoughts, Matthew reached up and untied the rag, letting his jaw hang slack. His mouth spilling open, displaying blackened gums and yellowed teeth, and more than a few maggots fell out onto the worn floorboards below, wriggling and squirming. Edward glanced down at them, his face impassive despite the wave of nausea that washed over him. He looked at Matthew who sat back again, rag still in hand, and spoke in a low, gravelly voice, barely above a whisper.

"I...it is good to see you again, brother," he said, and the sharp smell of decay wafted through the room, causing

160

Edward to wrinkle his nose.

"It is not good to see you, Matthew, for I do not believe that I am indeed seeing you," Edward replied stoically.

"Brother, do you doubt your own eyes? What do you think I am?" Matthew replied.

"When we last spoke, nearly half a decade past, you were a living man. When you were infected you were dispatched and cast out. How you come to be here now, sitting as you are in front of me in my bedroom is impossibility. I do not, nay, will not, believe it."

"So logical, so calculating. Do not even trust your senses?"

"Not in this matter. I have seen you die, rise again, and put down a final time. You are nothing but a figment of my overtired imagination, perhaps a dark spot on my brain caused by stress or food poisoning. No, I do not believe you are real," Edward said, but before he could clasp his hands together in triumph Matthew rose, grabbed his brother's robe and pulled him to his feet with ferocious strength.

"You dare gloat? You do not believe this real?" With that Matthew pulled his brother off the ground and dangled him like a doll, shaking him violently. Fear filled Edward's eyes now, and Matthew's cracked and discolored lips curled back in a tight smile.

"Good. I think you understand now just how real I am," he said, releasing his brother who dropped to the floor, crumpling and immediately curling in a defensive position.

"I did not come here to hurt you, brother," he said, sitting back down again. "Get up, please."

Edward looked at him, still visibly frightened, and slowly sat back in his chair.

"Then what did you come here to do, pray tell?"

"To warn you."

"Warn me? Of what?"

"Of what awaits you," the zombie said matter-of-factly. "What lies on the other side?"

"The other side of what?" Edward asked.

"Life. The wall. Both of which are unknown to you, which is why I am here. I am your guide, your intercessory, a portend."

"And what do you foresee for me, dear brother?" Edward asked, unsure of his desire to hear the response.

"You are witnessing your very fate, if you do not change your ways, Edward. You too shall roam the earth, damned for all eternity, killing indiscriminately, and forever seeking living flesh to satiate you. You will find no comfort, no rest, and no peace. This existence is a ceaseless, unliving hell, and you are headed for it straight away."

Edward felt a tingle along his spine as his dead brother's milky eyes seemed to pierce him with his unblinking gaze.

"What would you have me do?" he asked the zombie.

"This town is well-fortified, and there are many good people within its walls. You pass each without giving a second thought to their well-being, their comfort, or their futures," he explained. "You do not assist them in their defense, you have not enlisted in the militia, and you have contributed nothing that would even come close to saving a

162

life. We may have sprung from the same mother, Edward, but in life we were two entirely different people altogether."

"Yes, I remember Matthew; you were the inventor, the savior, the one praised for your efforts and sense of duty. But do not forget that we were both owners in the same shop, both profiting handsomely, and I do not recall you ever turning down a single coin for your troubles," he responded.

"DO NOT MOCK ME!" Matthew roared, his voice rattling the window glass in their panes. Edward shrank back, trying to sink as deeply into the chair's cushions as he could.

"We profited from those ventures, but that money was to be reinvested in the town. By defending these townspeople, we defended ourselves. By boosting creature comforts, we made all of us comfortable. It is for the greater good that the power plant was built, for the protection of all that we erected the great wall. But you, after I was gone there was no one to watch you, to shame you into demonstrating even the merest shred of compassion, and you sat in that shop, alone, counting coins, scurrying to and from this house like a rat, leaving your nest only to feed off of the townspeople. And it will be like a rat that you die, alone, full of disease, turned into a ghoul who will be hunted, put down like a rabid animal, before you can infect anyone else."

"But brother," Edward protested, "that very thing happened to you, and you were magnanimous in your lifetime. How can I, whom you clearly view as the more wretched one, escape such a cruel fate?"

"I will tell you, as that is the reason for my visit. It is not yet too late for you to absolve yourself, to turn over a new

163

leaf here in the land of the living. There is but one chance for you now." Matthew's voice echoed in Edward's head, the gravity of the situation silencing even his thoughts.

"You will be visited by three zombies, creatures such as me, with sense enough to reason and voice enough to convey meaning," he continued. "They will appear to you one after the other, so prepare yourself. You should expect the first to arrive when the clock strikes one."

With that, the zombified corpse of Matthew Oremor slowly rose, retied the rag around his head that held his jaw tightly in place, and backed away from Edward towards the door. He slipped out of sight into the darkness beyond and his brother could hear shuffling down the stairs below. Just then the window blew open, the wooden shutters flapping like a wounded bird's wings. Edward rushed over to shut them and when he turned back the door was firmly in place, whole and undamaged, the doorjamb unblemished, and the key in the lock just as he remembered, right below the dull brass knob which remained unturned.

Blinking once, twice, he shook his head in disbelief. "Bah," he began, but, thinking better of it, stopped speaking altogether. Exhausted and mildly confused, he flopped onto his bed and fell into a deep sleep with all of his clothing still on.

***

Edward awoke in absolute darkness, his sole companion the ticking of a watch hidden in his vest pocket. With a line of sweat across his forehead, he opened his eyes wide, feeling his face muscles strain as he tried to take in more

164

light. His hands shook as he fumbled with the matches atop his bedside table, and after a few tries struck a small flame, lighting the end of a half-burned candle sitting upright in a brass holder.

He glanced around the room and everything appeared in order, the door was still sealed tight and the windows shut, and the chairs held no ghoul, whether real or imagined, and he felt relieved. Reaching for his watch he pulled it out and checked the time. It was two minutes until one o'clock! He sat on the corner of his bed, the candle slowly dribbling wax into the holder, and stared at the hands ticking slowly around the face, transfixed by the tiny movements of the sweep second hand as the hour rapidly approached.

In no time at all it was one o'clock and Edward looked around the room like a bird at a feeder, twisting his head back and forth to try and catch this visiting zombie in the act.

"Ha! Nothing, Matthew! I just knew you were a rotten bit of meat in my soup, and not my brother returned from beyond the grave, beyond the wall."

"I wouldn't be so sure," something murmured from outside the reach of the flickering candlelight. It was a low voice, like a hiss, and Edward recoiled as it slithered into view. Framed only by the weak light, it appeared to be a bloated mockery of human form, a glistening, pale, pasty maggot wrapped in rags. Its eyes were swollen shut into dark slits, the nose barely recognizable, and its mouth was swollen, the lips like two fingers wrapped around a wound. As it moved closer Edward could see its flesh taking on a greenish tinge, like something rotten through, some unknown

165

contagion festering beneath the surface.

"Come Edward, there is no time for your fear," it rasped. "You must accompany me, for I have much to show you, and very little time." An elbow jutted out and waggled like bait, but Edward did not want to take it.

"Creature, couldn't you simply tell me what I need to know? I promise to listen, enraptured, but please, I dare not touch you..."

The sentence hung, unfinished, as the zombie reached forward with uncommon speed and gripped his arm like a vice. "Do you think your brother would allow harm to befall you?"

Edward shook his head hastily, although he looked wholly unconvinced. The zombie pulled him from bed with incredible force and hurled him towards the window. Edward threw up his arms and squeezed shut his eyes, convinced he was about to be killed, instead, he felt the warm sun on his face.

He looked around and found himself staring down at his childhood vacation home, a small cabin near a pale blue lake. The water ran along the edge of the forest, which was beginning to transform its green into brilliant hues of red, orange and gold. He spotted a car speeding along the winding road to the house, churning up great clouds of dust. It was unmistakably his parent's old station wagon, and he knew immediately what year this was, what day, what hour. It was the beginning of the end for Edward and Matthew Oremor.

"Are we...really here?" he whispered, and the zombie shook its head.

"No, we are only witness to things already gone by, and nothing you do or say can alter a thing. There is no way to interact with your past, but hopefully, you will see something you missed."

And, just as the zombie predicted, Edward watched it all unfold again: he and his brother being herded out of the vehicle by his mother, helping her drag their father's injured body inside the cabin, desperate to heal his wounds. They had narrowly escaped the city, now overrun by hordes of mindless, craven, and flesh-hungry undead, and safe out here, miles away from what used to be considered civilization. They thought they were safe, and they would have been right, if they only understood what a bite meant for the living.

That night, Matthew and Edward had to put down both of their parents and were at once orphans in this strange new world. Matthew seemed to take it better than Edward, at least outwardly, but Edward, being the eldest, if only by a few years, bore the brunt of the responsibility and all of the feelings which go along with the heavy duty of killing those who had sworn to protect you. They had lost their innocence that day, and never fully recovered.

The zombie saw the single tear escape Edward's eye, run down his face, his lip, and into his mouth.

"Regretful, wasn't it?" the creature hissed.

"My only regret is for those little boys, old before their time. The world is harsh, unforgiving, always has been, always will be. You have to be tough to survive, and should give no quarter to those who would force you to be unguarded."

"Oh really?" it replied, a bemused look playing upon its disfigured face as it watched Edward pretend to scratch as he wiped away the wetness.

"Yes," he replied, clearing his throat loudly. "And are we done here, wretched creature? Have we no better place to be?"

"I could easily ask the same of you," it answered, and gripped Edward's arm once more as the world around them winked out and only darkness remained.

***

Edward sat upright, looking directly at what appeared to be an old wrought-iron bench. He glanced around and spotted other benches, all similar in construction. There were small shrubberies and flowerbeds here and there, and the odd lamppost sprang up like metal weeds. Realization flooded his face as Edward realized where they were, the park in Old City, the name of the place Edward and Matthew moved to before ending up in New Town, the fortified home where he spent his days counting coins.

"Yes," the zombie said with a hiss, "welcome back. Just as you remember it, I presume?"

The creature pointed a grub-like finger across the park to a pair walking along the pathway, winding around the benches. Edward knew who they were even before they came into focus; it was himself, a much younger version of course, walking alongside a beautiful young woman. They wore the fashions of the day, tight fatigues tucked into heavy boots, a large holster for weapons and a vest with pockets. Their hair was clipped on the short side, although the young lady's was tied up in a ponytail held with a bright red ribbon, and around their necks they wore whistles, for warning and communication. This was the time referred to as The Gloaming, and people were still exceptionally cautious and vigilant, even in heavily populated areas. Especially in heavy populated areas.

Both young people were gesturing wildly, and Edward watched his younger self point and shake his arms and stomp his feet. He remembered this conversation, all right. As if lip reading, Edward heard in his head what Barbara was saying, even from this distance, and sharp pain seemed to stab his heart.

"You must know, Edward, this isn't something I desire, but something which must be," she protested. "How can you, of all people, not understand the utter importance of this?" The tears in the corner of her eyes sparkled like jewels in the pale, fleeting sunlight.

I understand perfectly the dangers of doing this. The militia has enough help; they do not need you too. Stay with me, out of the fight, safe in my arms. We will comfort each other, my dearest," he said, but it was clear from her expression that Barbara's mind was already made up.

"That is the path of cowardice," she replied, and held up her hand as Edward tried to say something, "and impossible. How can we stay here in comfort knowing there are innocent people still running for their lives outside of this city? We should, no, we must, protect them. I love you Edward, but even if you won't fight, I have to."

"But Barbara, is it cowardice to love you so much that I

wish no harm befall you?"

"No, that is not the cowardice I speak of. The militia command is on their way to aid and rescue a band of travelers, and you would rather hold my hand and sit by a hearth. That is cowardice," she said with finality.

Edward glanced over his shoulder at the sound of heavy footfalls. "They're coming to get you, Barbara. I beg you, one last time; will you change your mind?" But even as he pleaded, cajoled, begged, she would not be moved by his entreaties and left the park with the squadron. Edward sank onto the bench with closed eyes and clenched teeth, refusing his body the tears it wanted so desperately to shed.

***

Edward picked his head up from the blanket covering his bed, the ticking of the watch loud in his ears. The bloated, hissing creature was gone, and so was the nightmare of his haunted past, long buried deep in his mind. The candle had burned quite low, but was still giving off a small patch of light, and Edward checked the watch, which read two o'clock, on the nose. He squinting, trying to peer through the gloom and noticed a darker patch detach itself from the surrounding shadows and fill his vision. It was the blackened body of a wretched thing, a zombie so badly burned you could see through its flesh to the bones beneath. Muscles and ligaments were fused with skin and cloth, its face a horror show. Eyeballs protruded from sockets, skull showed through cheeks and jaw line, its nose had been burned clean off; it looked more skeletal than human.

"Oh you wretched thing! Even after the previous

170

visitations, I still have trouble looking at you and seeing the human you once were." It stared at him.

"Well, let's get this over with then, creature. Take me where you need me to go!" No sooner had the last syllable finished than Edward felt a great gust envelop him, as if caught in a sudden windstorm. When his vision cleared he was standing in a great battlefield, body parts strewn as far as he could see. There were a few men hunkered down, hunched over the dead and moaning, keening, *'no doubt wailing in mournful repose,'* he thought. He turned to the zombie, who was still staring straight into his eyes.

"Go to them," it said in a squeaky voice, its voice box probably damaged in whatever caused its gristly demise. Edward shuffled across the cracking asphalt and husks of automobiles hastily pushed aside and realized that this was a road, now the scene of warfare. As he got closer he could see that these men were not mourning, but feeding, squatting over their kills like animals and shoving great quivering hunks of meat and gristle into their open maws. Their hands and faces were coated with a thick layer of slimy gore, stringy bits of flesh dangling from their teeth.

Edward put a hand up as if to hold back the bile, but contained himself. He turned back toward the zombie who had led him here.

"What would you have me do?" he pleaded, and the creature responded, "Look."

He turned back and spotted a small group of zombies feasting on what seemed familiar bodies. The corpses were dressed in tight fatigues, and many were wearing vests, and

171

one of the zombies who were wrist-deep in a chest cavity was also wearing a similar outfit, only she had...she had...

At the sight of the red ribbon still tied neatly around the zombie's ponytail, Edward did indeed retch, opening up his mouth and letting the meager contents of his stomach spill onto the ground. Barbara did not stop, she did not turn around, and there was no reaction from her. Edward did not expect there to be, but even still, he could stand it no longer.

"Wretch! Leave me alone! I want nothing more to do with you!" he yelled as he waved his arms in the zombie's face.

"As you wish," the creature replied, and suddenly Edward was wrapped in wind once again, but when it died down he was not transported back to his room, but rather, all alone on the cobblestone streets of New Town, where the twinkling of search lights glinted down from the massive wall which stretched out of view. Edward breathed a sigh of relief that the horror was over, he would not have to witness his former love as a mindless flesh-eater. But he could not unsee it either; he knew that much for certain.

It seemed strange out here on the streets as he picked his way back home, there didn't seem to be anyone about, not even night watchmen. He was starting to get spooked, even after all he had been through this night, and it was then, as he turned down a darkened alleyway, that a shadow detached itself from a wall, blocking his path. It was a hooded figure, its face an aphotic void, and Edward could see nothing within.

"You must be my final visitor," Edward said flatly, drained even of curiosity. Pulling his watch from his vest he

172

glanced at the time. Three o'clock. The shadowy figure simply pointed, a mangled and mostly fleshless hand poking out from underneath the robe, in the direction of the main gate.

"I suppose I should go, creature, to witness what might become my fate if I do not change my ways, as my brother suggests. Although from what I have already seen, there is not much hope for me, is there?" he asked, knowing he would get no response. The zombie kept pointing, so Edward trudged off, hoping this final vision might at least end quickly.

The gate came into view, each door towering over Edward, nearly three times his height, locked tightly. There were only a handful of people who could operate it; most of them were night watchmen, who seemed to have disappeared. Suddenly, Edward spied a small figure scurry to a ladder attached to the wall and begins climbing with great haste, heading past the antechamber that contained the gate opening mechanism. Matthew had described it once to him as he was finalizing the design, but Edward was not interested in how it worked; only that it did work, and that the town would pay handsomely.

The figure moved quickly along the top of the wall, pulling at what appeared to be ropes lashed to great iron lanyards, and at once knew these to be balloon tethers. He saw them lift slowly and blot out swaths of stars as they floated away from their posts, as the figure descended once again, heading directly into the antechamber. Edward could feel the gigantic gears grind and click as the doors began to open, and it was then he heard the moans and grunts coming from just beyond.

It took a moment to realize what was happening, but then it dawned on him, these were the dead, about to swarm into a sleepy town who would never know what hit them. Once better prepared, they had grown complacent; the wall which protected them these many years had instilled a defense within them that was hard to take away. The figure in the antechamber hit the ground just as the doors finally opened, allowing the mindless hordes access to feast upon the sweet innards of this great shelled beast of a town.

Edward turned back towards the shrouded zombie who accompanied him, silent and ugly as a church roof gargoyle. He begged and pleaded, asking him to explain what this meant.

"Is this the lesson I should learn? If I do not change my ways, the entire town might suffer? What have I done that is so despicable that so many might suffer for it?" But the zombie was unmoved, remaining silent. It only pointed its thin, bony digit once again, this time aimed directly at the other hooded figure, the one who opened the gate and unleashed this hell onto the town.

"What, creature, what?!" he cried out, even as he walked ever closer to the figure. Finally he was so close he could touch him and longed to pull open the hood, but knew this was a futile gesture. However, the figure did it for him, reaching up to expose its face, and Edward finally allowed his body the tears it had waited for all night. The figure underneath the hood was Edward himself; still gazing out at the walking corpses he had allowed into this sanctuary, a look of contentment spread wide across his face.

174

Edward wept openly, distraught at what he had done, will do, whatever. It did not matter; it was a shattering thought to think he could house such evil, such malice for his fellow man, scarcely believing the darkness in his soul could drive him to such extremes.

"Why?" he cried, looking back at the hooded figure in horror, "why would I do such a thing? Can you not illuminate me; show me where I may have stepped off the path, so I may work to redeem myself from this waking nightmare?"

The creature raised its arm and gestured with an outstretched hand, and Edward followed himself as he scurried from the wall like some frightened insect, only to have his way barricaded by two strong-looking night watchmen.

"Where do you think you're going?" the larger of the pair asked.

"Did we just witness you unlocking the gate and releasing these things into our town?" the other guard probed.

"You must have mistaken me for someone else," Edward replied curtly, and tried to push his way past them. They grabbed him, each holding an arm, and pushed him to the ground, where he landed hard on his backside.

"Start talking, before we toss you off the wall!" the guard barked.

"If you insist," Edward said, and futilely straightened his dark cloak, smoothing out the fabric with shaking hands. "This place you call home is nothing but a cemetery. We do not live here, we await death. Those which dwell outside the wall are not things, as you refer to them, they are us."

175

"There is not a shred of humanity in them!" the larger night watchman spat. "They wish only to destroy us, and will not stop until they have stripped us of what we are."

"Nonsense! They are our friends and family, taken from us before their time, and now, despicably, we fend them off. We should embrace them, and allow them embrace us, to end this suffering and bring us back together. Forever," he finished softly, looking down at his hands. "I have had to put down my family, my love, and watch as everything was taken from me. Why continue on like this?" he whispered.

The two guards looked at each other knowingly and with a nod hoisted Edward to his feet as he mumbled to himself, chin buried in the folds of his cloak, and began dragging him towards the wall.

Without warning, a small herd of zombies shambled into view from around the corner, and the night watchmen tossed Edward to the ground again like a heavy sack and turned tail, heading to the town center for reinforcements. Edward just sat there, softly weeping and sniffling while the zombies milled about for a minute or two. They did not view him as a threat, or a meal, or...anything. They shuffle away slowly, dragging their feet in search of fresher, more active quarry.

"Wait!" he shouted to them, "don't go! Do not leave me like this! You must help me!" he continued, but not a one heeded his pleas. "I can't be left here like this," he said, "I do not want to live in a world such as this anymore. I want to be at peace, I want to be with my loved ones," he sobbed. As that Edward pushed against the ground to stand up, the other

Edward just stared, the hooded being at his side silent as the grave.

He realized now how short-sighted he had been, how selfish to wish for not only his own death but for the death of the townspeople as well. Now that he saw his future his true heart shone through, and he understood why he had been so absorbed in his work. If he saw these townsfolk as real people, and got close to them, he could lose them, like Matthew and Barbara, and he did not think he could take it. So he closed himself off, erected a wall around his heart, and like the town, waited to die. But he did not want that, not anymore. He only wished to live, to live, damn it all! To have that chance once again, that was what Matthew's visit held, he was certain.

Edward laid a hand on the robe of the creature next to him. "I understand now, kind ghoul, what I had become, and glad that you have shown me a different path. Thank my dear brother for me, and please, take me homeward once more," he said gently, wholly unprepared for what followed.

"Tell him yourself," a familiar voice growled from behind him, and when he turned, he saw Matthew and the other two zombies standing side by side in the alleyway.

"Ah, brother, I wanted to thank..." he began, but did not finish. The hooded figure gripped the arm still on its own and held Edward as the others approached, oblivious to his struggles to wrench himself free.

"Resistance is futile, brother," the dead man said to him in measured tones. "Did you not want this very thing mere hours ago?"

"No, not anymore!" Edward shrieked as the zombies

closed in on him. The bloated, pale zombie from earlier tore at his chest, ripping his clothing away as the badly burned zombie began to gnaw at his stomach, biting a hole in his flesh, lapping at the blood and gore which appeared. The figure which held him snapped back its head and the hood fell down around it, revealing a disfigurement which nearly made Edward pass out. Its face had been torn away and the eyeballs were no longer there, but rather empty, bloody holes in its head. The lips had been torn off and the gums and teeth were visible, very visible, as it tore into Edward's neck, ripping a chunk of flesh and muscle away as his screams filled the night air.

***

Everything was black, and for an instant, Edward thought himself blind. Then, imperceptibly, light pierced his eyelids, slowly filling his eyes with diluted sunlight that streamed in from the window. He sat up, rubbed the sleep from his eyes and looked around. The candle from the night before was melted and frozen in a motionless puddle around the holder, and he was still wearing the same clothing, his nighttime robe still neatly draped over the chair beside the bed.

"Was that all a dream?" he wondered aloud, and suddenly realized how very thirsty he was. He got up, feeling a little woozy, and hobbled over to the window, threw up the sash and peered between the iron bars to the cobblestones below. It was a glorious day, the dazzling sunshine throwing the beauty of New Town into sharp relief, making Edward ebullient to be alive. He glanced down at the watch, still hanging by its chain from his vest, and noticed the time and date.

"One day!" he exclaimed. "Those creatures had done it all in a single night, of course they would, of course they could," he prattled to himself. "They can do anything! Even my dear brother, who cared enough to give me a second chance, conjured for me my deepest desire!" He drew in a breath and pushed his face towards the window once again. He spied a young woman wandering down the roadway, just passing by the house when Edward called out.

"You there! Good Madam! I beg you, what day is it?" he asked, already feeling the warmth of a good-natured attitude brimming just behind his eyes. He could imagine it now, nearly skipping down the lane as children followed along behind, handing out gifts and trinkets, foodstuffs galore, the lavish party he would host, the improvements to the town he would fund, oh how joyful he would be, how happy to be alive!

He caught himself and looked down once again, shaking himself from his reverie. The woman moved closer to Edward's house now, and he could make out her torn fatigues, her ripped vest, and her hair falling out of a ponytail, the red ribbon still securely in place. Barbara turned and looked up at Edward with a gore-encrusted face, her white eyes rolling in her head. She hissed loudly, drawing the attention of other zombies who stepped out into the street, their heavy footfalls unsteady on the uneven cobblestones. He saw his brother Matthew and his bluish-white pallor, his parents a little ways behind him, he even thought he spotted the other zombies who had visited him in that fugue state before ducking his head back from the window.

Despite the pounding of his heart against his ribcage, he still felt ecstatic. He had gotten his wish, his family was here, and he could be with them for as long as he lived, and even longer. He went back to the opening, a smile on his lips, and could almost swear that Barbara's dead face reflected happiness as well, as she ran her torn tongue over cracked, yellowed teeth in base hunger, and lurched towards his front door.

ABOUT THE AUTHORS

Alex Azar is an author born and raised in New Jersey. His first submission acceptance was in NorGus' very own *Look What I Found!* anthology. He's also been published in NorGus' *Undertaker Tales*, Post Mortem Press' *Isolation*, and Static Movement's *Obsession* and *School Days* anthologies.

Mild-mannered librarian by day, **Jason M. Bloom** haunts the stacks awaiting the cloak of night, when he can finally go home and start writing. His muse and beautiful wife Shannon helps keep the demons at bay, or draws them out, depending on the project. His works have been published in the literary magazine Shoreline, the Pill Hill Press anthology *365 Daily Bites of Flesh 2011*, *Dead History II* from Living Dead Press and in *Strange Tales of Horror: An Anthology* by NorGus Press.

With seemingly alchemical powers, the stories penned by award-winning author **Crystal Connor** are amalgamations of horror and science fiction, truth and fable, past and present. Using her ballpoint like a magic wand she inscribes tales of terror that you won't soon forget.

Brandon Cracraft lives in the historic district of Tucson, Arizona with his boyfriend and a black cat. His short stories have appeared in several anthologies including *Monster Party, Attack of the Fifty Foot Book,* and *Look What I Found.* He has also written plays, screenplays, and articles.

Dale Elster lives in Auburn, NY with his wife Jannette and their two children, Brady and Maryn. More of Dale's work appears in the NorGus Press anthology, *Look What I Found!*, as well as Collaboration of the Dead's zombie anthology, *So Long, and Thanks for All the Brains!*

Jason "J. Rodimus" Fowler was born in the summer of 1976 and hails from Raleigh, North Carolina. He has had a passion for horror and the absurd since he was a small child, which he blames in part on his babysitters, who just happened to have been Monty Python and Rod Serling -via- the Electric God/television. His twisted tales of fear and retribution range from battling hordes of the undead, to true love among demon fodder.

Robert Freese is the author of the zombie novel *Bijou of the Dead*, the paranormal book *Paranormal Journeys* and the horror/sci-fi novella *The Santa Thing*. His most recent short stories have appeared in CD Publication's *In Laymon's Terms*, the Norgus Press anthologies *Strange Tales of Horror* and *Look What I Found!*, the Pill Hill Press anthology *Daily Bites of Flesh 2011: 365 Days of Horrifying Flash Fiction* and the charity anthology *The Undead that Saved Christmas: Vampire Edition*. His first scripted comic appeared in the charity anthology *The Undead that Saved Christmas Volume 2*. His collection of horror stories *13 Frights* will be released in 2012 by StoneGarden.net Publishing.

Allan Izen is a free lunch writer living on the windward side of Oahu. He's managed to peddle fifty-odd (some very) short stories and a dozen or so articles.

Thomas M. Malafarina (www.ThomasMMalafarina.com) is a horror fiction writer from Berks County, PA. He has published three novels, *99 Souls*, *Burn Phone* and most recently, *Eye Contact* and two short story collections called *13 Nasty Endings* and *Gallery Of Horror* through Sunbury Press of Camp Hill, PA. (www.Sunburypress.com). He has also published a collection of single-panel cartoons called *Yes I Smelled It Too: Cartoons For The Slightly Off-Center* through Sunbury. He has written dozens of short stories, which have been featured in numerous anthologies as well as on internet audio podcasts.

Marc Sorondo lives with his wife and daughter in New York. He has had work published by Pill Hill Press, Wicked East Press, Post Mortem Press, Blood Bound Books, UnEarthed Press, and NorGus Press.